BLUE SCHWARTZ AND NEFERTITI'S NECKLACE

A mystery with recipes

BLUE SCHWARTZ AND NEFERTITI'S NECKLACE

A mystery with recipes

Betty Jacobson Hechtman

Brown Barn Books
Weston, Connecticut

Brown Barn Books
A division of Pictures of Record, Inc.
119 Kettle Creek Road, Weston, CT 06883, U.S.A.

www.brownbarnbooks.com

Blue Schwartz and Nefertiti's Necklace
A Mystery with Recipes
Copyright © 2006, by Betty Jacobson Hechtman
Original paperback edition

The characters and events to be found in these pages are fictitious, although some of the places where the events take place are real. Any resemblance to actual persons living or dead is purely coincidental.

Library of Congress Control Number 2006924148

ISBN: 0-9768126-3-0, 978-09768126-3-0

Hechtman, Betty Jacobson
BLUE SCHWARTZ AND NEFERTITI'S NECKLACE:
    A Mystery with Recipes

Printed in the United States of America

To Burl and Max

You guys are the best

Acknowledgements

I want to thank Nancy Hammerslough for her enthusiasm and excellent editorial suggestions. Thanks to Jessica Faust for all her time and patience.

Joan Jones helped me find my voice and put me together with my great critique friends Linda Bruhns, Jan Gonder and Jack Warford.

Where would I be without my cheerleaders Roberta Martia and Judy Libby?

Thanks to Sarah Levin and Rachel Hyatt for testing the recipes and giving them their seal of approval.

I'm sure my parents Helen and Jacob Jacobson must be clicking their heels with joy in heaven.

I appreciate my brother David Jacobson for taking me on star hikes in the country when we were kids, and for all the computer advice.

Thanks to Max Hechtman for being the best son ever and bringing so much happiness and adventure into my life, and for advising me on seventh grade dating.

And of course, thank you to Burl Hechtman for his unfailing love and encouragement, and the endless rides to the airport.

Lastly, thanks to Hyde Park, Chicago, a neighborhood with a unique spirit that will always be home no matter where I live.

Chapter One

I know what Professor Albany is going to say before he opens his mouth. I've been babysitting for the Albanys for a couple of months, and every time he gets ready to take me home, he says the same thing.

I gather up my books and papers, watching him. He's kind of short for his age, and I'm tall for mine, so we almost see eye to eye. Like always, he's wearing one of those preppy outfits—blue oxford cloth button down collar shirt and gray slacks. To me anyway, he looks like a newscaster instead of a University of Chicago professor. Most of the people around here look more rumpled. As soon as Mrs. Albany pays me, he turns to her and says, "I better hurry and take Blue home before they tear down her building."

He always says it like he thinks it's some kind of joke, and laughs to prove it. It's true my building's really old and my parents are worried it's going to get torn down, but I don't think it's funny. Any more than when he started calling me Bruise. See, he said, Schwartz, which happens to be my last name, comes from

1

the German word for black. So, like my name is really Black and Blue—like a bruise. He laughed a real lot over that one. Luckily, he forgot about it pretty fast. Too bad he can't do the same with his cracks about my building.

But I am not going to let it get to me. I need all the babysitting jobs I can get. My family has zero extra money. The only way I am going to ever get any good cooking tools, those black shoes with the bows at Marshall Field's or a computer is if I get the money myself. And there is everyday spending money for things like after-school pizza at the Medici and bus fare downtown.

I put the money in my school bag and take my jacket off the chair. That's when something really weird happens. When I go to put it on, out of nowhere this gold bracelet falls out and hits the floor. I look at it totally surprised and wonder where it came from. The Albanys both stare at it, then at me.

"That's my bracelet," Mrs. Albany says.

"Blue, do you want to explain?" Professor Albany says, looking at me with one of those raised eyebrow expressions.

"Huh? What do you mean explain?" I say confused.

The bracelet is still on the floor like some kind of tiny gold sparkly worm.

"Explain what you're doing with my wife's jewelry?" His mouth goes into this phony kind of smile, and his voice sounds sing-songy like when people talk to little kids. "I know it must be tempting to see nice things..."

Then it hits me like a brick what he's getting at. It must have looked like it came from my jacket. He thinks I was trying to steal it. It feels like my insides just dropped to the floor. Is he crazy? Me, steal something? Never. I have to make them understand there's some kind of mistake here.

I'm so totally shocked. I tell them twice I have no idea how the bracelet got there. They have to believe me. "You can't think I took it?" My voice sounds squeaky, and my cheeks feel hot.

"I probably dropped it in the chair when I was rushing to get ready, and it just snagged on Blue's jacket," Mrs. Albany says picking it up.

"That must be what happened," I say quickly.

Professor Albany agrees, but something in the way he says it makes it seem like he isn't sure. "Okay, Blue, we'll give you the benefit of the doubt, this time."

Even though I'm angry at being accused, I'm still relieved. I can't afford to lose any customers. For once, I'm even glad when he goes back to his bad jokes about my building as he drives me home.

"Oh, good, it's still standing," he says in pretend surprise, stopping in front.

I go through the front hall, which is lit by a naked light bulb. There's no buzz door or carpet on the stairs, but it feels like home. I storm up the stairs, still upset the Albanys could think I would steal something.

As I pass Mrs. Bliss's door, it opens.

"Blue, I hear Chef Randy is making a Pfannkuchen tonight. It's some kind of giant baked pancake," she says, peeking out. She has white hair and eyes so blue I sometimes think she wears those colored contact lenses. We almost always watch Chef Randy together.

The TV is already tuned to the cooking channel when I go in. We don't have cable, so the only way I can watch it is at Mrs.

Bliss's. I usually love to watch Chef Randy. But after what just happened, it's hard to care that he has all the ingredients lined up in those neat little bowls. Or that he's wearing a white apron with a hand towel hanging over it. I'm staring at the screen but not really seeing all his great cooking equipment. Well, maybe I do notice that blue KitchenAid® mixer. But my mind keeps going back to what Professor Albany said about giving me the benefit of the doubt *this time*. What if something like this happens again? It gives me the creeps to think about it.

I try to make myself pay attention to Chef Randy. He's using his super powerful stainless steel blender for the batter. He takes one of his many spatulas to scrape the little bowls full of flour, eggs, sugar and milk into the blender. He even has a bowl for the vanilla extract. Real vanilla extract. That's the only kind he uses. Then he takes another bowl with a chunk of butter and scrapes it into a pan. He must have tons of those bowls.

Whenever I cook, I have to keep stopping to measure stuff and then put it in the mixing bowl. It would be so nice to be able to line everything up the way he does and then just keep adding the ingredients. It would be nice to have one of those great electric mixers too, and all those neat spatulas. All my tools are just make-do. One of my goals in life is to become a successful soufflé maker. So far my specialties are simpler things like oatmeal cookies and popcorn balls.

Mrs. Bliss notices right away that I'm upset. I have already decided not to tell my parents about the thing with the bracelet. My mother always tells me I need to be able to fight my own battles. It's part of her plan to make my brother and me able to make it on our own. My parents are a lot older than my friends' parents, and they could die any time. She doesn't exactly mention

4

the die thing. She just says they might not be there forever, which I think is the same thing.

I do tell Mrs. Bliss about the bracelet and all of Professors Albany's stupid comments.

"Well, things are just going to hell in a hand basket, dearie," she says. "What is that man doing accusing you of anything? And this building is just fine."

Mrs. Bliss is worried about our building being torn down, too. Her daughter is always telling her she shouldn't live alone and ought to go somewhere meant for old people. If the building goes, Mrs. Bliss is afraid she'll have no choice but to move to one of those places her daughter keeps finding.

"Isabel brought me this brochure from Cozy Manor today," Mrs. Bliss says, showing me the cover. It's all green hills and looks like a cemetery.

"Why does she think I want to spend my time getting driven around in a golf car? I'd rather have this." Mrs. Bliss and I look around her living room. She has all kinds of neat stuff to look at. My favorite is the lamp next to the rose print chair where she always sits. It has a big glass shade that looks like nothing special when the light is off, but when it's on, you can see this whole scene of mountains and a river. She has some others that have shades made up of little pieces of colorful glass, like stained glass windows. They're much prettier when they're on, too.

Her mantel is loaded with photos and her teacup collection. She says the cups remind her of trips she took all over the world. Most of her furniture looks like it's been used a lot, except for the Queen Anne green velvet sofa with the wood trim. It's only for special occasions and looks like new, even though it is really very old.

And unlike the boring square rooms in the Albanys' town house, Mrs. Bliss's living room has bay windows with curved glass, and this thing called a pocket door that slides out of the wall and divides her living room into two rooms. You can even see places on the wall where there were once gas lamps.

Chef Randy comes back from a commercial. He finishes showing the baked pancake preparation. Then he goes to the oven. This is my favorite part. The way he opens the oven door and says "Woohooza!" just before he takes out a finished one. The pancake looks so good, I can almost smell the buttery baked aroma.

Next, he says he's going to show how to make strawberry sauce to go with it.

"Oh, dearie, I better call upstairs and let your parents know you're here," Mrs. Bliss says, getting up.

A minute later, she comes back shaking her head.

"Your mother said those Albany people just called and want you to call back immediately."

A loud "uh oh" goes off in my head.

Chapter Two

"So what exactly did they want?" my friend Yvonne asks the next day. We're just coming out of school, and I have just finished telling her the story of the bracelet and how Professor Albany thought I took it.

"It was Mrs. Albany, and she wanted me to babysit the kids this afternoon."

"That's good then," Yvonne says. She knows how much I need the work. "They must have forgotten all about the bracelet thing."

"Yeah," I answer, but then my attention gets pulled away. I stop Yvonne, and we watch as Shane Calavedo comes out.

He just came to Ray this year. He's from somewhere in Southern California. He always wears Hawaiian shirts, khakis and sneakers. He even wore them in the dead of winter. I just love his hair. It's kind of long and that golden color like all the surfer guys have.

"Hi," I say as he passes. He sort of looks up.

"Hey." He nods at me and keeps walking.

Yvonne has to punch me to get me moving. "What exactly do you find so wonderful about him?"

I am still amazed that he said "hey" to me and am too stunned to answer.

"I forgot my key *again*. Want to come with to get my mom's?" Yvonne asks when I come back to earth.

I still have some time before I have to pick up the Albany kids, and get unstunned enough to say yes.

Since Yvonne forgets her key at least a couple times a week, it's lucky Mrs. Johnson works just a few blocks away at this place we both call the mummy museum. Its real name is the Oriental Institute.

As soon as we get to the gray building, we go up the stairs two at a time, and pull open the big wooden door. It's usually pretty quiet on weekdays, but today there seems to be a lot of stuff going on. Some men are bringing in huge wooden boxes and carrying them into one of the exhibit halls. I can't see in because its glass doors are covered over with dark red curtains. There's a sign in front mentioning a new exhibit opening a week from Friday.

On top of all that, there are a bunch of people coming out of the regular exhibit hall. Yvonne's mother sees us when we come in and waves. She's unpacking stock for the Suq, which is what they call the gift shop.

"We got a lot of new things in for the special show," she says, holding out a box of little cat statues made out of gold. Or gold coloring anyway. Mrs. Johnson says they're just copies.

"What do I have to do to get you to remember your key?" she says to Yvonne. She's kind of laughing when she says it, so you call tell she isn't really mad. And you can tell by the way she hugs her.

That's when I notice this touristy looking couple by the cash register stop checking out the miniature pyramids and start checking out Yvonne and her mother, I guess because they look so different. See, Mrs. Johnson has long silky blond hair and really pale white skin. Yvonne is a lot darker. She's kind of the color of coffee with a real lot of cream, and her hair's toasty-brown and kind of wiry.

I've never seen her father, but she told me he's black. Her parents got divorced a long time ago, and I think he moved to some other town. She only hears from him on birthdays and stuff.

Yvonne says it's only people from outside our neighborhood who make a big deal about the difference between her and her mother. Around here, there are so many people in so many colors from so many places, it's hard to even figure what's different.

While her mother goes to get her key, Yvonne and I look at the glass case of jewelry they have for sale. They have a lot of copies of old stuff, and some cool things like this pair of earrings that look like cobras about to bite somebody.

Then we go into the regular exhibit hall. We always go to the same place. Past the big mummy boxes, there's a glass case with a little boy mummy. He's all wrapped up. It's creepy and cool at the same time. Across from him, there's a mummy bird. It's a hawk or something and still all wrapped up too. Then there's this little baby crocodile mummy. It's unwrapped enough so you can see its shriveled little head. Yvonne and I both go yuck and then run back toward the Suq laughing.

Mrs. Johnson is waiting with the key, and I tell Yvonne I have to go.

I rush across the campus, dodging students pouring out of all the gray buildings. The grass is turning a nice green, and the lilac bushes are flowering and smell wonderful. I'm supposed to pick up Matthew and Luke at Botany Pond. Professor Albany might give me a hard time, but his kids are great.

The boys come running as soon as they see me. I'm surprised to see they're with a guy with glasses and dark hair that looks like it was styled by the wind.

"Hi, you must be Blue Schwartz," he says coming toward me as the boys each grab one of my hands. "I'm Zack Mason, Professor Albany's teaching assistant, and temporary babysitter." He gives me the stroller like he's really glad to get rid of it. I drop my books in the basket.

"Mrs. Albany went downtown," he says, handing me the keys to their house. "And Professor Albany's giving a lecture. Standing room only. You know people come from all over the world to study with him."

Zack keeps on talking about Professor Albany, saying how important he is around there and how he's sooo brilliant. Zack makes him sound like some kind of brainiac god, and I should be honored to babysit for him.

I don't pay much attention. Except when he gets to the part of how the Albanys get to travel all the time and just went to Egypt.

"I wonder if he saw any mummies?"

Zack rolls his eyes like I am some kind of idiot. "I don't think so." He picks up his backpack and walks away shaking his head.

Matthew and Luke want to go around Botany Pond before we go home. The lily pads are growing back from the winter. The green circle leaves look like you could walk on them. Luke takes a step to try, but I grab his hand and pull him back just in time. I make sure to hold both of their hands as we go around on the cement ledge. I point out a few goldfish you can see between the lily pads.

When we get back by the little bridge, I get the stroller, and Luke climbs in. He's only two and a half and still needs to ride. Matthew's four and walks next to us as we head for their house.

Mrs. Albany has left a note about giving them some graham crackers and peanut butter. It also mentions milk and bananas.

I love their kitchen. They have a side-by-side refrigerator that gives you ice water from the door. They also have built in counters and cabinets. Our kitchen just has a big old table and instead of cabinets, we have a pantry. Somebody said our building used to be a hotel which is why the bedrooms and kitchen are all pretty much the same size. I think the pantry used to be a closet because it has drawers.

I can't believe it. The Albanys have the same blender as Chef Randy.

I make the snacks Mrs. Albany mentioned, but the boys just push them away. Then I get an idea. Last week Chef Randy did a show about smoothies. All of them had great names. Things like Strawberry Splash, and Banana Bonanza. He said the names were important. He said "They lift them from the ordinary."

"How would you like me to make you guys a special drink...a...a Blue's Blizzard?"

They both nod and get excited. I guess anything sounds better than what they have.

I pull chairs over for them to watch. There are some dessert bowls in the cabinet that are just the right size. I measure some milk into one, and cut the bananas into another. I find some frozen blueberries in the freezer and pour some in another bowl.

"This is the secret ingredient," I tell them in a whisper, taking out a brown bottle of genuine vanilla flavoring. "And it has to be the real kind." I pour in a teaspoon full in the last bowl. Then I take off the top of the blender and start adding the ingredients. When everything's in it, I turn it on. I explain about running it until all the bumps of blueberries disappear.

"Woohooza!" I say, pouring the smoothie in two glasses and giving one to each of them. They drink some right away and get it on their faces.

Just then, the door opens and Mrs. Albany and another woman walk in. They each have a shopping bag from Marshall Fields. Mrs. Albany looks up the stairs and smiles at the boys. Her eyes seems to stop on the drinks in their hands. I notice her smile disappears, and she looks like she just swallowed a storm cloud.

I hear that "uh oh" voice going off in my head again.

Chapter Three

Mrs. Albany rushes up the stairs and snatches the drink right from Luke's lips. Of course, he begins to cry.

"Blue, what have you given them?" She looks over the counter and sees the plate of graham crackers with peanut butter. She grabs it and hands one of the crackers to Luke, or at least tries to. He pushes it back at her and reaches for the glass of Blue's Blizzard in her hand. The cracker falls sticky side down on the floor.

Meanwhile, her friend drifts into the living room and starts calling out questions about what is this and that. I lean over to where I can see in the other room. She's looking at the big case with the glass doors. I checked it out the first time I babysat. The shelves are filled with little statues and things like pottery with pieces missing. It even has lights on the inside.

"Is this Nefertiti's necklace?" Mrs. Albany's friend asks, pointing at something.

"Be there in a minute, Carolyn," Mrs. Albany calls. She looks at the glass in her hand and then at me. "What exactly is this?" She says it like it's some kind of poison.

I give her the ingredient list, and then what does she do but smile and get all excited about how I actually got Luke to drink milk and eat fruit. She rushes to give him back the glass. She even asks me to leave the recipe. I go to clean up the cracker on the floor, but she says she'll take care of it. I'm suddenly like the hero of the day.

Luke and Matthew keep on drinking as she pays me. They're comparing their blueberry moustaches and laughing.

"Blue, we are going to need you on Friday—for the afternoon and evening. You'll have to take the boys out for a few hours and then come back here," she says as I pick up my school stuff. She goes on to tell me they're having a cocktail party at their house, and want the boys out of the way. After I bring them back, the Albanys and their guests are going to some University thing. I say "yes" right away. An extra long job means extra big bucks.

When I get home, I divide the money in the boxes on my dresser. One is for everyday expenses like after-school pizza at the Medici with Yvonne. The second has my computer fund. I peek in the box, hoping somehow the few lonely tens have multiplied into a wad of bills. No such luck.

I really want my own computer. Then I could use it whenever I want to. My brother is supposed to share the one we have with me, but he never does. It's in his room, and he's always using it or about to every time I ask.

The third box is for the pair of black shoes with the little heels I saw at Marshall Field's. They have perfect little bows and would work for any party. That box has only change.

All my clothes and things are hand-me-downs or from rummage sales. My mother always brags how she never had to buy me a winter coat until I was eight. They always came from other kids who outgrew them. I don't mind getting used stuff, but just once I'd like a pair of shoes that were mine first.

My mother is taking her after-work-before-dinner nap. We pretty much have hamburger meat with a different name every night. If it has tomatoes, Italian spices and is over thin noodles, it's spaghetti. If has tomatoes and green peppers and is over thick noodles it is subgum. If it has beans and tomatoes it's chili, and if it has tomatoes and is in one piece, it's meat loaf. I take a sniff and recognize the spicy spaghetti smell.

My father is grading papers on the dining room table that is in the living room. I want to call Yvonne, but as soon as I get the phone and try to stretch it to my bedroom, which used to be the dining room, my brother comes out of his room. He says he's studying and my phone call is going to make too much noise.

Eric's in high school and spends hours and hours on his homework, which he insists he can't do unless it's quiet. He's the great brain hope of the family and all everybody talks about is what college he should go to and how he can get a scholarship.

"Blue, why don't you make your call later, when Eric is finished?" my father says from the living room.

It looks like I have no choice but to do my homework before I do my dinner job. I make the salad. It's always the same—iceberg lettuce, grated carrots, cucumber slices and a few tomato wedges with this dressing my mother makes from an envelope. I wish she'd let me try one of Chef Randy's Splendid Salads. He uses all kinds of different lettuces, and things like sun dried tomatoes. He mixes the dressing himself with all these different kinds of oils and vinegars.

I don't even get to watch my cooking show later. Mrs. Bliss's daughter is visiting and probably brought another one of those brochures from some place called Happy Meadows. For the rest of the week, I only get to see Chef Randy once. It's classic week and he does his "Woohoozas!" over macaroni and cheese the night I watch. I didn't know you could make it without a box.

I babysit for the Mansards once, Shane Calavedo says "hey" to me twice, and Miss Hooper assigns a report on a food item. On Friday, Yvonne and I splurge and get pizza slices at the Medici. We take the big cheesy slices across the street to Bixler playground and find a bench by the fountain. I plan to just eat mine and go right to the Albanys', but Yvonne keeps picking at her piece and staring at the ground.

"Hey, what's up?" I ask her as I wipe the cheese grease off my chin.

She takes a while to answer, and I start getting nervous. Mrs. Albany made a big deal about being on time, since I have to get the kids out of there before their guests arrive.

"My father called," she says at last. Then she tells me he moved back to Chicago and lives in Kenwood, which is the neighborhood north of Hyde Park where we live. "He wants me to come over on Sunday and spend the whole day."

I don't know what to say. This is the first time she ever mentioned seeing him. And it's pretty obvious by the way she's hanging her head this isn't happy news. She says the rest so softly, I have to lean next to her to even hear.

"He's got a new wife and a baby." She picks up her head and looks right at me. "That means I've got a stepmother. And there's more. I saw a picture. She's black. My father tried to put his hand over the phone, but I heard her talking. She called me his half-baked daughter."

"Geez," is about all I can say. Yvonne's life is certainly a lot more complicated than mine. Suddenly having Eric-the-brain-and-silence freak for a brother doesn't seem so bad. I tell her to call me the minute she gets home from the visit. I feel like a jerk for running out on her, but I've got to get to the Albanys'. She is still sitting on the bench as I walk away.

Chapter Four

Everything is crazy at the Albanys' when I get there. Professor Albany is more dressed up than usual in a dark suit. He just lets me in and hurries back into the living room. I notice him fussing around the big glass case.

The guy I met at Botany Pond comes through. His hair still looks like he uses the wind for a comb. "Hi. Blue, isn't it?" he says. He reminds me his name is Zack and he's Professor Albany's assistant. He's carrying an ice bucket out of the kitchen and looks pretty dressed up, too. He has a sports jacket over his jeans. Whatever the Albanys have going must be a pretty big deal. Even Zack seems pretty nervous.

Mrs. Albany sweeps down the stairs with Matthew and Luke. She's all done up in a gray dress and jacket outfit, and her rust-colored hair is in a new poofed up style. I can't believe what she's got on her feet—the black shoes with the bows from Marshall Field's I want so badly. Like I said, they could work for any kind of party—or age, I guess.

"Why don't you just take the boys out now," she says. Luke and Matthew kind of hang back, like they have figured she is trying to get rid of them.

"How about going to the Museum," I say in what I hope is a bright, inviting voice. "We can go to the coal mine and there's the train and the plane you guys can go on..." All of a sudden they get it. No matter what is going on at their house, it can't match the Museum. Everybody just calls it the Museum, but its whole name is the Museum of Science and Industry. It's walking distance, and the best place in the world to take a couple of squirming boys.

We cut through Jackson Park and then turn a few blocks before the beach. The Museum is this huge building with domes on top, and statues of women holding up part of the roof.

Before we even get inside, Luke and Matthew want to go everywhere at once. One says the "space shuttle," then the other yells "submarine." I mention the baby chicks hatching and get instant "no's" from both of them. As soon as Matthew sees the real Zephyr train when we first walk in, he wants to go on it, but Luke points upstairs and keeps saying plane. He means the United airplane stuck onto the balcony. It does this whole take off and landing show. And then both of them remember the coal mine and want to go there.

The coal mine wins. We start up the escalators, and ahead, I see a familiar Hawaiian shirt and khakis. Shane Calavedo lounges against the side of the moving stairs, talking to some kid I recognize from eighth grade.

They stop when they reach the top and are still there as I help the boys off the escalator. I wait until Shane glances my way.

"Hey." I put on my best smile.

"Hey," he says back.

"What's up?" I ask. Matthew and Luke aren't happy with my stopping to talk. They each grab a hand and start to pull. Shane holds up a notebook. "School project. I got to do a report on the heart." He points across the balcony toward the walk-through-sized heart.

For a moment nobody says anything, and I think he and his friend are just going to walk away. I just say whatever comes to my mind first.

"I'm babysitting." I pull Matthew and Luke closer as evidence. I don't mean to, but I start rambling on about the Albanys' party and having to take the kids out.

"Albanys' huh? Yeah, Sophia's going to the do," Shane says with kind of a laugh. "She's my mom," he adds, when I seem confused.

I am totally knocked out that he calls his mother by her first name, but I try to act real cool. "What a coincidence. Your mom, I mean, Sophia, being at the Albanys' party."

He nods. His friend kind of hits him on the arm with his notebook and gestures across the balcony. Matthew and Luke start pulling for real now.

"I gotta go," I say.

"Yeah, me too."

I wish him good luck on his report, and let myself be pulled toward the coal mine. I have this goofy kind of happy feeling as we take the elevator down. I just love how he called the party a "do." It's so cool. It must be a California thing.

I've been to the coal mine a million times. I used to think the elevator really took you below ground instead of just to the basement. Matthew gets all excited about the coal on the walls, and the miner's train we get to ride on. Luke grabs onto me and hides his face when they do the demonstration of exploding gas. Afterwards Luke wants to go to what I call old-fashioned street. I kind of look around for Shane and his friend, but don't see them as we head for the dark, cobblestone street. You'd think you were outside at night a long time ago. There are store fronts and real cars with those funny big tires. I always look at the display window that has the high-button shoes and corsets. It makes me glad I didn't live then. Luke is more interested in the ice cream parlor, which is really real. We get ice cream and drinks and sit at one of the marble tables. I check people going by the window for Shane Calavedo, but don't see him.

"I want the submarine," Matthew says as I wipe his face.

"Sorry, guys, we got to go." I take their hands and lead them out of the ice cream place. Practically next to it is this replica of an old dentist's office. It gives me the creeps to even look at that straight chair and all those metal things with points.

"Plane, plane," Luke whines and points. Matthew says I promised we could go on the train. I am saved by a museum guard who announces it's closing time.

The walk back is harder than the one there. Both kids are tired and not excited about our destination.

Mrs. Albany lets us in as her friend Carolyn and her husband walk out. Between telling them she'll see them later at the Quadrangle Club, Mrs. Albany tells me to take the boys downstairs to the play room. The minute we get down there, they say they're hungry and I creep up the stairs to the kitchen. I had expected the party to be over, but there are still some people in the living room. They all seem to be hanging around that big case with the lights. I'm curious if one of them is Shane's mother, and I wonder what the big deal is on the shelves. I decide to make peanut butter on apple slices for Luke and Matthew. As I go for an apple, I kind of lean toward the living room to see if I can get an answer to both.

"Do you know where the broom is?" Zack asks, coming in the kitchen.

I point toward the tall cabinet on the end. Maybe I should just ask him who's who at the party and what everybody is so excited about. But before I can open my mouth, he's gone. So, I have to go back to my own information gathering.

"My, but it's a beautiful necklace," a woman says.

Professor Albany's voice gets a puffed-up sound. "I knew you would appreciate it." I think he says her name, but I can't quite hear it. He could have said Sophia.

Just as I am peeking around the wall to get a look at her to see if she looks like Shane, Mrs. Albany brushes past me as she comes in the kitchen. She picks up an empty tray, and then turns as a man and woman stick their heads in. They say "good bye" and the woman says something about "that piece being exquisite." Some other people are leaving too, and I wonder if Shane's mother might have already left.

I feel like I am invisible. Mrs. Albany is so into her party and guests, she doesn't even seem to notice me. She takes the tray back into the living room and starts picking up glasses and snack plates. I make another attempt to check out the party for Shane's mother.

By now, there are only a few people left. I recognize Mrs. Mansard. I babysit once in a while for her. She's standing right next to the big case, and the doors are open.

"What do you think?" she says, turning toward her husband like she is modeling something. Before he can answer, Professor Albany jumps off the sofa. "The necklace is to look at only," he snaps, reaching around Mrs. Mansard's neck. She doesn't look very happy and tells her husband they ought to go. "Phillip," Mrs. Albany says, shaking her head. He apologizes to everybody and makes some lame joke about being too protective about the latest addition to his collection. "Sorry, sorry, I don't mean to be the death of the party," he says putting the jewelry piece back in the case. "Anyone for another drink?"

"We'd better go or we're going to be late," Mrs. Albany says, adding some more glassware to the tray.

"You're right," Professor Albany says and then calls to someone across the room. "Why don't you ride with us, Sophia?"

It's got to be her. Sophia Calavedo. I follow where he's looking, half expecting to see a woman wearing a Hawaiian shirt and khakis. Not exactly. She's got on one of those wear anywhere-black tank dresses, and lots of silver jewelry. Her hair is the same honey color as Shane's. So that's his mother. It's not like I'm going to rush up to her and introduce myself or anything. I just watch her for a little while.

Content that I figured out which one's Shane's mother and that everybody seems to be gaga over some new necklace, I start to slice the apple.

I'm busy spreading peanut butter when all of a sudden there is a loud crash in the living room. I drop the slice I'm working on and rush in. Mrs. Albany is standing looking down at the tray and a lot of broken glass. It's like everybody's frozen for a second and then comes to and starts rushing around.

Zack has the broom and dustpan. Somebody else gets a bag for the glass. Professor Albany tells everyone to hurry. It seems like everyone is moving, trying to clean up the mess. It's like absolute pandemonium. Mrs. Albany keeps saying she doesn't know how she dropped the tray as she hustles me in the kitchen and quickly gives me directions for the boys' dinner. Before she can even finish, Professor Albany comes in holding her coat. Then they all leave.

I finally take the snacks downstairs. Matthew and Luke have fallen asleep in the middle of the floor.

I take the opportunity to go back upstairs to check that all the glass is gone. Then I wander over to the display cabinet to see the necklace everyone was making such a fuss about. I look over each shelf. All I can find is an empty piece of velvet.

Chapter Five

"Phone call for you," my mother calls, poking her head in my room. Before I even sit up in bed, she has already gone back to her vacuuming. She always cleans the apartment Saturday morning. I stumble out of bed and go for the phone. We're probably the only people in the world that don't have a cordless one or cell phones. My parents think they give off some kind of death rays and cost too much, too. We just have one phone with a very long cord. I pick it up and start walking down the hall to get away from the noise.

"Hello." I do my best to get the sleepy sound out of my voice.

"Blue, this is Professor Albany. You must come over here immediately." His voice sounds strange, and I wonder if there's some kind of emergency. Especially since Mrs. Albany is the one who calls when they need me to babysit.

I try to find out what's going on, but he won't tell.

"Just come over here. We'll discuss it when you get here." He is almost yelling when he says it.

I get dressed quickly and head for the door.

"Where are you going so early?" my mother asks over the sound of the vacuum cleaner.

I tell her I'm going to the Albanys'. She doesn't hear me, and I say it louder.

My brother-the-brain opens his door. He's wearing ear plugs and holding a book. "What's going on?"

I just shake my head and rush down the hall to the living room. My father's drinking coffee and grading papers at the dining room table. I call where I'm going as I hurry out the front door.

Mrs. Bliss opens her door as I pass. Sometimes I wonder if she just sits by the door listening for footsteps.

"Don't forget, Chef Randy is doing 'Spotlight on Soy' today." Her blue eyes really do twinkle when she smiles.

I barely stop on my way down the stairs, but tell her I'll be there for sure.

The few blocks to the Albanys' house go by in a blur.

Professor Albany opens the door before I can even ring the bell. He looks like his voice sounded—like he's about to explode.

"Come in," he says, almost growling the words.

As I go inside I get a bad feeling in my stomach, like when you're on a elevator going down too fast.

Mrs. Albany is in the kitchen. She doesn't look very happy either, but not as bad as her husband.

Luke and Matthew hear me and start to come up from the playroom, but their mother orders them to go back downstairs.

I can't take the suspense any more. I swallow, feeling like I have a ping-pong ball in my throat. "Is something wrong?'

"Is something *wrong?*" Professor Albany repeats. His eyes open real wide and his mouth stops in this mean grin. "I wanted to call you last night, but my wife talked me into waiting. I don't know why I listened to her."

"Phillip, remember anger is bad for your blood pressure," Mrs. Albany calls. Her mouth is locked in a straight line. "Maybe you should let me handle this," she offers.

"No," he says sharply. Then he turns back to me.

Professor Albany tries to calm down, but he still has that about-to-explode look.

"Young lady, there is *definitely* something very wrong." I hate it when people call me "young lady." It's always followed by bad news. This time's no different.

"A necklace disappeared last night." Professor Albany just stares at me.

I start to feel a little better. "Oh, you mean the one everyone was talking about?"

He nods, and then I tell him when I looked in the glass case after they left, it wasn't there.

"Maybe it dropped behind something when someone put it down," I say, glancing toward the living room.

Professor Albany looks me in the eye. "We both know that isn't what happened, don't we? Just like that bracelet didn't really just happen to get caught in your sweater."

Suddenly, it's like someone just punched me in the stomach. "You think I took it?" I look up toward Mrs. Albany holding her morning coffee. Her expression isn't any kinder than his. "How can you think I took it? I don't even know what it looks like."

Professor Albany hands me a picture. I'm expecting something with diamonds and maybe rubies or something. Instead it's made out of gold-colored beads with tear-drop shaped kind of charm things that are red, blue and turquoise. Maybe it's the color combination, but it reminds me of the jewelry they sell at the mummy museum gift shop.

I tell them I didn't take it, but he puts his hand up. "Blue, you have one week to return it."

"But...but..." I try to explain.

"And if it isn't back by the end of the week, I will have no choice but to turn the matter over to the police."

My insides feel like they've evaporated, and I am afraid I'll just fall over. I try to protest again, but Professor Albany just repeats his warning.

This can't be happening. How can they think I'm a thief? All the way home, I have this horrid daymare of being taken away in a police car. Would they put me in jail? It's too creepy to even think about.

Mrs. Bliss hears me go by and opens the door. She knows right away something is wrong.

"Dearie, you look pale as a glass of skim milk. What's the matter?"

I tell her I'll come downstairs in a few minutes.

My mother has turned off the vacuum cleaner and is sitting at the table with my father when I walk in. They are talking and shaking their heads. I hear the dreaded words summer and money and what are we going to do? Every year there is the same problem. Both my parents work in schools and are off all summer which means no paychecks. Summer vacation is only a month away, and they're starting to get worried. How can I tell them about the missing necklace? They have enough to deal with, and besides, my mother's always telling me I have to take care of my own problems.

"Come in, come in," Mrs. Bliss says when I come downstairs a little later. "You still look peaked, dearie. What's the matter?"

I sit in a slump in front of the TV. While she clicks on the Food Channel, I tell her what happened.

"Oh, that is trouble," she says when I finish. "Such silly people, to even think a good girl like you would steal anything."

"I don't know what I'm going to do."

Mrs. Bliss clucks her tongue and pats my hand. "You just tell those people you had nothing to do with its disappearance."

The opening of Chef Randy's show begins. There are all these funny drawings of cooking things while they list the people that work on the show. I don't want to hurt Mrs. Bliss's feelings, but that isn't much help. I could tell the Albanys I didn't take it until I am as blue in the face as my name, but they're not going to believe me. There's only one way out of this mess. I have to find out what really happened to the necklace.

Chapter Six

My mind is worn out from thinking about missing jewelry. I'm glad to forget about it for a few minutes and lose myself in Chef Randy's Spotlight on Soy. He shows this bowl of things that look like peas in the pod. He opens them and pops out what he says are soybeans. Then he holds up a plate with this white stuff that looks like a bar of soap, only it jiggles. He calls it tofu. Chef Randy picks up what looks like a milk carton. The stuff he pours out of it looks like milk, but he says it's soy milk. And he says you can use it just like regular milk, like on cereal or in cream soup or to drink.

"I wonder what it tastes like," I say to Mrs. Bliss. "Isn't it weird to think of a drink made from beans?"

"We could get some at the store, dearie. I was going to go anyway. Maybe you'd like to come along," she offers.

"Sure," I say, nodding. I go shopping with her all the time. She never exactly asks for my help, but I know she likes it. She walks with a cane and it's hard for her to carry packages or pull a shopping cart.

When the cooking show is over, I get the fold-up cart while Mrs. Bliss gets her coat.

As we are going down the stairs, her daughter Isabel is coming up. She has the same blue eyes as her mother, but hers are all worried looking.

"Mother, where are you going?" Isabel stops and glances back and forth between us and sees the fold-up thing under my arm. "Did you look at the booklet I left you on Sunset World? They have mini buses to take you shopping."

Mrs. Bliss keeps moving down the stairs. "Isabel dear, I can shop just fine here. As long as I have Blue, I don't need any mini buses. Besides, walking is good for you." She says it in a cheery tone. But Isabel gets an exasperated look, and when we get to the street, she goes back to her car.

I love going to the store with Mrs. Bliss. We make it an adventure. She's as curious as I am, so we always spend a long time wandering the aisles looking at all the exotic foods. Sometimes she buys the stuff we look at, and we taste it together. So far, we've tried almond butter, jalapeno jelly, parsnips and blood oranges.

Like always, we cruise the aisles of the Co-op, which is the major neighborhood grocery store. Between getting her regular groceries, we check out the huge selection of barbecue sauce and the new products section.

We have to ask someone where the soy milk is. They have plain, vanilla and chocolate. No matter how many times Chef Randy oohed and aaahed about how great it tastes, we're both not sure. So, we decide just to get an 8-ounce carton of the vanilla.

When we head into the produce department, a cart crashes into ours. I look up and see it's being pushed by Zack, Professor

Albany's teaching assistant. He's so busy looking at a display of oranges, he doesn't seem to notice he hit us. I try to move our cart out of the way, but he hits us again. The second crash finally gets his eyes off the oranges.

"Oh, sorry," he says absently. Then does a double-take when he sees me. "Blue, the babysitter," he says. He turns toward Mrs. Bliss. "Your grandmother?"

"Not exactly," I answer. Seeing him reminds me of Professor Albany which reminds me of my troubles. I get back the uneasy feeling. "Did you see what happened to that necklace at the Albany's last night?"

Zack drops a bag of Valencia oranges in his cart and shrugs. "Everyone was looking at it. I suppose Professor Albany put it back in the glass case."

"What's the big deal with it, anyway?" I say.

Zack doesn't seem very interested and keeps looking down the grocery aisle. "I don't really know. It's something the Albanys picked it up for their collection on their last trip."

"I could have saved them the plane fare. They have stuff like that at the Suq."

"Right, at the Oriental Institute," Zack says. "Why all the questions about it?"

I step a little closer to him and lower my voice. "The necklace is missing, and Professor Albany thinks I took it. Of course, I didn't, but, but—he said if I don't return it in a week, he's going to tell the police."

Zack's eyebrows go up and down. "He said that, huh? Well, I don't think you have to worry about him calling the police. He was probably just trying to scare you."

"Then he sure did a good job. I didn't take it. I really didn't," I say, looking him right in the eye so he'll see I'm telling the truth.

"Right, " Zack says.

I feel a little better. I figure he must know Professor Albany pretty well, being his assistant and all.

Mrs. Bliss tells him we're going to try the soy milk and invites him to join us. Zack is very polite, but declines.

Then he says he's got to go and moves on. Mrs. Bliss watches him push his cart into the salad dressing aisle. "That boy needs a comb."

We finish shopping and head for the checkout.

"There now, don't you feel better," Mrs. Bliss says as I unfold the cloth cart and help the box boy put the groceries in. "That young man seemed to think you had nothing to worry about."

"Maybe he won't call the police, but I don't like someone thinking I stole something."

"That Professor Albany is a silly man to jump to conclusions. It probably just got mislaid. I bet it will turn up," Mrs. Bliss says as we head for home.

I hope she's right.

Back at her place, we unload the groceries.

"Well," Mrs. Bliss gestures toward the carton of soy milk. "Shall we, dearie?"

Whenever we have one of our "tastings," as she likes to call them, we always make an event out of it. This time, instead of just putting it in ordinary glasses, she takes down two crystal goblets and pours some soy milk in each. We each take one and go into her living room. We sit on her best piece of furniture, the green velvet Queen Anne sofa.

"Well, here's to you," Mrs. Bliss says, lifting her goblet to touch mine.

We clink glasses, smile at each other, and go for it. It doesn't taste like milk, exactly, but it's creamy and sweet. Pretty amazing, considering that it came from a bean.

"I think we've found a winner," she says draining her glass. "We've got to try the chocolate next time."

When I finally go upstairs, the apartment is clean. Only my room is still a mess. I spend the afternoon making it match the rest of the place. I try my best to think about other things while I'm cleaning, but the necklace situation keeps coming up. Even if Zack is right, and Professor Albany won't really call the police, he still thinks I took it.

The only good part is I manage to squeeze in enough thinking about other things to come up with a great idea for my school project.

Chapter Seven

"**M**y weekend was horrible," I say when Yvonne and I finally connect on Sunday night.

"Not as horrible as mine," she says through the phone.

I have dragged our one phone as far as it will go, which is not quite as far as my room. The closest thing to privacy I can get is taking the phone in the closet next to my room. I am scrunched on the floor between my sneakers and my winter boots. It's the only time I'm glad I don't have many pairs of shoes.

"I bet you didn't have someone talk about you when you were right in the room," she continues, daring me to match it.

"Well, you didn't get accused of stealing." I have to keep my voice low. All I need is for my brother-the-brain to come complaining about noise and hear what I'm saying.

"But you didn't find out you have a wicked stepmother. That woman is just bad. She kept giving me this evil eye all the time they were showing me around their apartment. They got one that takes up a whole floor. My father showed me a room they're fixing up and said it's going to be mine. And then, right where I could hear, she tells my father she thinks I might be a bad influence on their baby. She says she doesn't want me teaching him *my* ways" Her voice suddenly goes soft. "His name is Ricky, and he's so cute." Then Yvonne sounds sad. "She would barely let me hold him."

I admit hers is pretty bad, but I have held out my worst for last in our terrible-off contest. "Yeah, but nobody threatened to call the police on you."

"Call the police on you?' She almost chokes on the words. "Okay, spill," she says, and I know I've won our contest. Like it's really such a prize, anyway.

Yvonne lets out these mini-gasps as I tell her about the necklace, the Albanys and my possible prison term.

"You've got to do something," Yvonne says when my story ends.

"I know. I just don't know what." My voice sounds like feet dragging on the sidewalk.

All of sudden, there is a knock on the closet door, and my mother says she needs to use the phone.

"Got to go," I whisper and get off the phone fast.

I make the mistake of thinking things can't get any worse. I should never do that because it seems like they always do afterwards. This time isn't any different.

It starts the next day when Miss Hooper goes around the room asking for the subjects of our food projects. When she hears what I've chosen, she looks surprised and not in a good way.

"Soybeans? Well, that's certainly different." When she says different, you can tell she means different weird, not different interesting.

She seems much happier with what the other kids have chosen. They all picked things like beef, cheese and everyday kind of food things. Since it turns out more than one person picked the same food, she decides to put them together and make the reports a group project.

She puts Yvonne with Samantha Parker because they both chose ice cream. Everyone else ends up in groups of two or three. After making a big deal again about how strange my choice of soybeans is, Miss Hooper says that since no one else had the same unusual idea, I'll have to do my report alone. Then she lets us break up into groups to start working. I end up just me with me.

And after school Yvonne drops a bomb on me over Medici pizza. I should have known something was wrong when she offered to treat. We usually only get pizza on Friday, and we always each pay for our own.

"Thanks for the slice," I say as we glide onto a bench at Bixler park. We have the playground to ourselves. Even though it's May and sunny, there's a cold wind off Lake Michigan. The fountain is going again after being turned off all winter, but the wind keeps blowing the water over the edge.

Yvonne puts her piece down. "I've got some bad news for you."

"Now what?" What could be left? I've been accused of stealing, threatened with the police, and treated like a freak in school. I suddenly lose my appetite.

Yvonne keeps looking down, holding onto the bench with both hands as she talks.

"Remember when we had the food project meeting?"

I give her a funny look. "Some of us had nobody to meet with."

"Sorry. Miss Hooper's an idiot. There's nothing wrong with picking soybeans. Okay, so when the rest of us had our meeting…

Samantha and I agreed that we would get together after school. I suggested tomorrow, and she said she couldn't because..."

Yvonne finally turns toward me. I get the feeling this is the bad news part coming up.

"She can't because she's babysitting for the Albanys." It takes a few seconds for what she said to sink in.

"What?" I yell. I jump up and start pacing. "But I've been their regular babysitter for months. I get it. It's the necklace thing again. It's totally unfair." And I realize it's even worse than that. The Albanys are, or maybe I ought to say were, my main customers. Right before my eyes I see my pocket money disappearing. The computer I've been saving for flies off in space, along with those cool black shoes with the bows from Marshall Field's.

Neither of us is very hungry anymore, and we dump the rest of our slices.

"I forgot my key again," Yvonne says as we reach 57th Street. "Want to come with to get my mom's?"

"Why not? It looks like I'm going to have lots of extra time," I answer glumly. "It's so stupid—that necklace probably just fell behind the shelves or something. There was so much commotion going on when Mrs. Albany dropped all those glasses," I say.

She nods in agreement.

"If I could just get a chance to check out the Albanys', I bet I could find it."

As we cross the street, I start to get an idea. We pass the Medici, then the bank. All the while I'm thinking. Just as we get to 57th Street Books, it comes together.

"I need you to do me a big favor," I say as we stop to see what's on display in the window. We have to look down. The bookstore is in the basement of an apartment building, and the windows are knee level.

"Like what?" She turns back to me.

"I'm thinking you could tell Samantha that you'll just stop by while she's babysitting. I could just happen to be with you. While you two are talking about ice cream, I could have a little look around." I give my best pleading look to Yvonne, and she breaks.

"Okay, but we better not let Samantha know what's going on."

"Of course." My mouth curves into a smile of relief. I will find the necklace and get my job back. That's when I notice the poster stuck to the bookstore window. "Wow, look at this." The poster announces an author evening with Sophia Calavedo. It says she's the author of the time traveler series and will be talking about her latest book *Cindi and Ahkenaton*. "I guess I didn't tell you. She was at the Albanys' party."

"Maybe she saw what happened to the necklace," Yvonne offers as we walk the rest of the way to the Oriental Institute.

"It doesn't matter because I'm going to find it tomorrow."

I follow Yvonne through the big wooden doors. As soon as we get inside, Yvonne walks toward the exhibit hall that has curtains covering the glass doors so you can't see in.

"My mom's working on the new show. They've got to rush to finish putting it together by Thursday because there's some big reception Friday night," Yvonne says before she knocks on the glass door. "I'll be back in a minute."

Somebody lets her in, and I walk over to the Suq. I check out the case with the jewelry. The cobra earrings are still there. Then I notice the necklaces on the other side. One of them is kind of like the one I'm supposed to have stolen. At least, the colors are the same. This one doesn't have the charms, but it has the same gold colored beads, separated by tube-shaped red, blue and turquoise beads. I keep staring at it, trying to imagine what could have happened to the one at the Albanys'.

"C'mon," Yvonne calls when she returns holding up the key.

We go back outside.

"Are you going to call Samantha? To set up tomorrow?"

"Are you sure it's such a good idea?" Yvonne asks as we head down University Avenue. My friend, the worrier, is backing down.

"If it was something with your wicked stepmother, I'd do it for you," I say hopefully. That kind of gets through to her, but she doesn't seem sold. University marks the border of the campus, and U. of C. students seem to be coming from everywhere. It's hard to talk to Yvonne when every few seconds we get separated by a bunch of people with backpacks and serious expressions.

"Samantha will never go for it, Blue. You better think of something else."

"You have to say something she can't turn down." I think for a few steps. "I know. Tell her you have to meet tomorrow since you only have until Friday, which incidentally, happens to be true," I say, nodding my head. "If I had to meet with a partner, I wouldn't want to wait until Wednesday."

Yvonne still doesn't seem sure.

"You could at least try."

The sun disappears and the wind switches. People always joke about Chicago weather being changeable, but it's no lie. By the time we reach 57th, both the weather and Yvonne's mind have changed. Clouds are rolling in now and the air feels moist and warm. And Yvonne agrees to call Samantha.

"You'll see. It's a great plan," I say as we get ready to part company. "What could go wrong?"

Remember how I said it isn't a good idea to say things can't get any worse because then they always seem to? Well, it isn't a good idea to say "what could go wrong" either.

Chapter Eight

"**O**migod, what's she doing here?" Samantha Parker says when she opens the door and sees me. She's talking to Yvonne, but her eyes are stuck on me. It's pretty obvious she isn't happy to see me. Like it's any surprise. I know she thinks I'm weird.

Yvonne kind of fumbles around. She's been nervous about doing this all day. At lunch, she tried to talk me out of the Plan. She's worried about getting in trouble. Yvonne is your number one good-girl type. I had to tell her about six times that my neck is on the line here. I have been accused of stealing something I didn't, and it is both terribly unfair and ruining my economic future. Finally, she agreed. But I can see Yvonne is having second thoughts—again.

"Omigod, is she trying to join our ice cream project?" Samantha has her hands on her hip with a real attitude thing going.

"Of course not," Yvonne says with a shake of her head like Samantha is being totally ridiculous. "Blue's got her own project. She just happened to be walking with me." I notice a little edge

47

in Yvonne's voice. I give her a thumbs up, for standing up to Samantha.

Samantha doesn't make a move to invite us in. The stairs are right behind her, leading toward the living room. My eyes keep going up there. It's so close but a million miles away at the same time if Samantha doesn't let us come in. All I need is a few minutes to search the place. I'm sure the necklace is just under something. The Albanys probably didn't even look very hard.

"All right," Samantha says at last. She walks inside, and we follow. "But we have to stay in the playroom." She takes us down the short flight of stairs to the big ground floor room that looks out on the tiny backyard.

I was so busy thinking about getting in the house, I forgot about Luke and Matthew. As soon as they see me, I realize it's a problem.

"Blue, Blue," Luke cries, running up to me. "Make a Blizzard."

Samantha turns, puts her hand back on her hip and glares at me. "What's going on, Schwartz?" Samantha likes to call people by their last names. She thinks it gives her an image.

Before I can say anything, Matthew has joined Luke in asking for a drink.

Now, it's my turn to fumble around. I certainly can't tell Samantha the truth.

"See, I do babysit for the Albanys usually," I begin, creating a story as I go. "But, I thought I had to go to the dentist today, so I told them I couldn't. But, the dentist got the flu and had to call off my appointment." It's not a great story, but not bad for a last minute make-up.

Samantha seems bored with the whole thing and drops her hand off her hip. "Whatever." Suddenly ignoring me, she gets out her notebook and pulls Yvonne off to the side. Matthew and Luke go back to watching their cartoons. And I look longingly toward the stairs. How am I going to get up there?

It hits me there is a way. "I'll make us all a Blizzard," I say making a move.

"No way." Samantha looks up from her ice cream discussion. "Mrs. Albany left snacks down here. And she made a big deal about me staying in the playroom."

Samantha and Yvonne go back to their work. This is awful. How can I get this close and not get to check out the living room? I jiggle from one foot to the other. There has to be some way. Then the obvious hits me.

"I gotta use the bathroom," I say, making my jiggle bigger. I don't wait for Samantha to say anything, but just head for the stairs. I hope she doesn't remember there is a bathroom on this floor by Professor Albany's office. I guess not because she just glances toward me and shrugs.

All right. I've done it. I go up the stairs three at a time. No time to waste. If I am gone too long, Samantha is going to figure something is going on.

The living room is sort of a rectangle, divided into two areas. Two ivory-colored couches with a glass table between make up one. The other has the glass case against the wall and a couple of chairs around a low marble table.

I crawl into the couch area first. Crawling seems the way to go. It's both a quieter way to move and easier to check under stuff. The couches have six cushions and two throw pillows each. I pull out all the cushions and check under them. Nothing. Putting them back is harder than pulling them out. They have to be in exactly the right place or they don't fit. In my head, when I thought about doing this, it only a took a minute. But the actual event is taking much longer, too long. I get more and more nervous as I keep having to switch the cushions around until I get them in right. It's a relief when I'm finally done.

I push my arm under the couches to check there, but only come up with a few dust balls. The only information I get from lifting the rug is that somebody needs to vacuum under there.

My heart seems to be beating faster and louder. And worst of all, I really do have to go to the bathroom now. I'm sure that necklace has to be around the shelves somewhere. The glass doors are locked this time. The empty velvet piece is still there looking lonely. I crouch further down and lie on my back so I can run my arm under the whole shelf area.

I try to look under as I run my arm along the cool floor. I start to worry about splinters and spiders. If only I had a flashlight. There is just a little more space to cover. I am so into what I am doing, I don't hear the door open and close or the footsteps on the stairs until it is too late.

"Blue!" A voice bellows. I don't have to turn to know who it is. I wish I could roll under the case and disappear.

"What are you doing?" Professor Albany yells. "The necklace wasn't enough for you? How did you get in here?"

By then Samantha, Yvonne and the boys have followed the noise upstairs.

"Omigod," Samantha shrieks when she sees me on the floor with Professor Albany standing over me.

He glares at her and Yvonne and turns to me. "Are they part of your gang?" he demands.

I'd like to tell him that if I had a gang I would never include Samantha, but what's the point?

"I didn't want to let her in," Samantha says, her hand back on her hip. She goes into the story about the ice cream project, putting in way too many "omigods," but Professor Albany isn't listening anyway. He grabs my arm and pulls me up.

"I just don't know what to do with you," he says, letting go now that I am standing.

I tell him the truth—again. That I didn't take the necklace. "I was sure it just got stuck under something. I thought I could find it."

Professor Albany doesn't seem to have heard anything I said. "Blue, you leave me no choice. I know I gave you until Friday to return the necklace. But after this…" He gestures toward me and the shelves. "I have to call the police."

He grabs my wrist and pulls me along as he heads for the phone.

Chapter Nine

I'm doing my best not to freak out as Professor Albany drags me into the kitchen. Samantha is right behind us, watching with horrified amazement. She keeps saying "omigod" over and over. Yvonne's face is frozen in kind of a shocked look.

Boy, have I made a mess of things. I didn't find the necklace. Courtesy of Samantha, the whole school will soon know I'm accused of being a thief. And Yvonne's worst nightmare has come true. She's in trouble.

I have to think fast. Very fast. Professor Albany is picking up the phone.

Pictures of me being taken away in a police car are floating through my mind. This is just too terrible to be true.

I may not be able to do anything to get myself out of trouble, but I can't let him blame Yvonne. Or Samantha, no matter how much I don't like her.

"They had nothing to do with it," I say quickly.

"How admirable. You're willing to take the whole blame yourself. But it doesn't change anything," Professor Albany says, pressing the on button. His mouth is squeezed in a mean expression as he punches in the first number. "Okay, Blue, I am going to give you one more chance. Where is the necklace?"

"I don't know," I say, feeling like the words are stuck in my throat.

Professor Albany shakes his head. "And you seemed like such a nice girl. But I guess, being so poor and seeing nice things, maybe you just couldn't help yourself."

I admit it looks pretty bad for me. My heart is banging so loud, and my throat has gone completely dry.

"Please." The word comes out like whisper. I can't believe I am going to say what I am going to say, but I am in an absolute corner. It seems like the only way out of this mess. "Just give me until Friday."

"Good girl," he says as he puts the phone down.

I didn't realize I had been holding my breath until it comes out in a gush. I take in a big breath of air. The vision of me riding off in a police car fades, and for just a moment I feel relieved.

But the relief doesn't last.

"Ah ha, so you finally admit you did steal it," Professor Albany says as his eyes light up. "But why do I have to wait until Friday. Go get it now." He's staring at me so hard, I'm afraid his eyes are going to burn a hole in my face.

My mind starts spinning, and I think I'm holding my breath again. "I can't," I answer, choking on the words.

"Blue, stop this nonsense. Just bring me the necklace." His voice has grown angry again.

"I need until Friday." I swallow hard.

"Do you mind explaining why?" he demands.

I want to tell him I'm not admitting to anything, that I don't have it, but what's the point? There is no way he's going to believe me, and he could still call the police. There is only one thing I can say, and for once it is the pure truth.

"I have to find it," I answer.

Chapter Ten

"**O**migod, who'd have thought you'd turn out to be a jewel thief?" Samantha sounds actually impressed. The three of us are walking away from the Albanys'. My heart is still pounding, and Yvonne looks pale.

"I'm sorry," I tell Yvonne again. "I thought it would be no problem."

Yvonne just shakes her head.

I am going to try and talk Samantha into keeping all this to herself, but it turns out I don't have to.

"I think we ought to keep this just to the three of us," she says, pulling us close to her.

"Blue, this whole thief thing is just too much image for you to handle. Nobody would believe it. You'd look like you were trying too hard, if you know what I mean."

I get it. I want to laugh. Here I am with one foot in jail, and Samantha's worried my potential bad-girl image will make the other kids think I'm hotter than she is.

"No problem," I say as she separates from us when we reach 56th. Yvonne looks relieved to see her go.

"What are you going to do?" Yvonne asks. We walk up to Bixler park and flop on a bench.

"What else can I do? I've got to find the necklace." The air has turned kind of chilly, and I pull my jacket around me. "I thought it was just lost. Now, it's pretty obvious somebody stole it. I've just got to figure out who and how to get it back."

Yvonne watches two kids play on the swings. "And I thought having a wicked stepmother was tough. What do you know about being a detective?"

"Nothing." I put my head in my hands.

Yvonne grabs my arm. "Me either."

I tell her I'm sorry I got her in trouble at the Albanys.

"It's okay." She squeezes my arm.

When I get home, my parents are having another one of their money conferences. Other than the soft rustle of their voices in the living room, the house is quiet. My brother-the-brain must be studying.

They both look up when I walk past. Maybe I should tell them about how much trouble I'm in. But as soon as I notice how worried they sound, even in whispers, and I remember the fight your own battle thing, I decide not to.

As soon as they see me, everything changes. They stop whispering and both put on phony looking smiles, like I'm supposed to think everything is under control.

"Blue, Mrs. Mansard called," my mother says. "She apologized for calling at the last minute and for it being a school night. She wants you to sit tonight."

I expect my mother to say I shouldn't because of school and all, but she doesn't. They must really be worried about money. She hands me the phone number. "You ought to call her right away. Before she finds somebody else."

I'm kind of surprised Mrs. Mansard called me. First, because they have a student living with them who babysits most of the time, and second, because not only were they at the disappearing-necklace party, but they live just two townhouses down from the Albanys. If they want me to babysit, it must mean Professor Albany hasn't spread the word I'm a jewel thief.

I hurry and call.

Mrs. Mansard apologizes to me for the same things she did to my mother. She sounds really happy when I say I can sit, and tells me she'll pick me up around eight.

I feel good for about two seconds, then I remember Professor Albany and my horrible afternoon.

"I'm going to Mrs. Bliss's to watch my cooking show," I say, heading toward the front door. I explain about what time Mrs. Mansard is picking me up. My father starts to say something when he hears how late it is, but my mother gives him one of her looks, and he stops.

Mrs. Bliss opens the door before I even land on the second floor.

"Hi dearie. C'mon in, I've got your chair all set up." Her blue eyes look even brighter than usual, and her white hair is in some kind of an updo held in place by tortoise-shell combs. Like always, she is wearing one of those colorful dresses her daughter gets for her at Wal-Mart.

No matter how hard I try, I just can't get into Chef Randy's show. I don't even care about the lineup of little bowls with all the ingredients. It barely registers that he is making pureed soup tonight.

"Aren't all those vegetables pretty?" Mrs. Bliss says. She points to the orange butternut squash. "I think that color is my favorite."

When I don't say anything, she turns toward me. "What's wrong, dearie? I know a stormy expression when I see one."

I try putting on a smile, but it doesn't work.

"And I know a phony smile, too."

I let the corners of my mouth sag and start to talk. "Remember how you thought that necklace was just lost? Well, I tried to find it." Then I tell her the latest episode in my life as a jewel thief.

She thinks I ought to tell my parents, but when I explain I can't because of all their own problems, she kind of nods like she understands.

"Tell me again what that Professor Albany said about calling the police."

I repeat how he dragged me to the phone, and then at the last minute didn't call.

"Well, sweets, I'm glad he didn't call the police, but with all the fuss that he was making, I think it's very peculiar that he didn't."

"Why do you think he didn't call?" I cringe just thinking of him starting to dial.

"I don't know, but there is definitely something fishy going on," she says, folding her arms.

When I tell her about babysitting for the Mansards and how they were at the party, she smiles.

"If I were you, dearie, I'd use it as an information opportunity."

Chapter Eleven

....

While I'm waiting downstairs for Mrs. Mansard to drive up in their navy-blue Volvo wagon, it hits me for the first time. If the necklace isn't lost, somebody else at the party had to have taken it. I keep thinking about what Mrs. Bliss said about the information opportunity. Mrs. Mansard has to know something, or have seen something, unless...could she be the one? I realize the next few minutes in the car might be the only chance I get to find out.

The honk of a horn gets my attention as the blue car double-parks in front of my building. The box-shaped station wagon doesn't seem like the kind of thing a jewel thief would drive. I'd think they'd go for some sports model with an exotic name like a Lamborghini or something. I run outside. It's still light out since it's almost summer, but it's an unwritten babysitter rule that you get picked up any time after six.

"I'm glad you could sit, Blue," Mrs. Mansard says as I shut the door. "Eleanor, that's the student who lives with us, had to go somewhere, and this meeting is really important."

I smile, but inside I'm looking at Mrs. Mansard in a new way—as a suspect even if her car doesn't fit. Like always, she has that artsy look. She's big on scarves and unusual pieces of clothes. Tonight, she's wearing khaki slacks and a cream-colored shirt with an orange and brown jacket that looks like it came from another country, like maybe Mexico. She's got a yellow scarf wound around her head and lots of jewelry. I check it out with new interest. She notices me looking at her thick silver bracelet.

"I just love unusual jewelry," she says, offering me a better look at the bracelet. It has heart-shaped holes that have been filled with pieces of amber.

I know I should start asking her questions instead of just admiring her bracelet, but I don't know what to ask.

"That was some party the Albanys had, huh?" I say as an opener. She just kind of uh huhs. "What did you think of that necklace?"

We're at a stop sign and Mrs. Mansard turns toward me. I am surprised to see there is suddenly a whole lot of expression going on in her face. "What a beautiful piece. I thought the combination of the turquoise, carnelian and lapis in those teardrop dangles was exquisite."

Then suddenly, like she caught herself, she stops.

I remember how she tried it on at the party and hope bringing it up will keep her talking. "I thought it looked really beautiful on you."

She sneaks me a smile. "Didn't it. It would be so gorgeous on a white linen dress. I don't care whether that story he told about it is true or not. If it were mine, I'd wear it, not keep it in some

silly glass case. But Phillip Albany and I don't see eye to eye…"
She seemed to catch herself again and stop talking.

I want to keep her talking, and besides, suddenly I realize what a strange place it is to keep a necklace. "Why is it in that case, anyway?"

"Oh, you know Phillip, well maybe you don't, but he likes to collect…" Her voice trails off as she pulls the car in front of their house. I want to try and get her to finish what she was saying, but their front door opens and Eleanor, their live-in student, comes rushing out. Mrs. Mansard gets out of the car and starts talking to her and never finishes the sentence about the glass case.

I hadn't really thought about it before, but it is a strange place to keep a necklace. And why wasn't anybody getting to wear it? This isn't going well. So far, I've ended up with more questions than information. Mrs. Mansard didn't even act like she knew the necklace was missing.

The outside of the Mansards' townhouse is just like the Albanys', but inside it's completely different. The Mansards is filled with unusual stuff. Things like a coffee table made out of glass over a neat looking tree stump. They have an oval purple velvet couch covered with all different needlepoint pillows, and chairs that are all different styles.

Mr. Mansard comes down putting on his sports jacket with his jeans and joins his wife. Then, leaving behind a cloud of their combined colognes, they go out the door.

Their daughter Boo—her real name is Elizabeth Ann, but everybody calls her Boo—is asleep already, so there isn't much for me to do. I forgot to mention that in all their unusual stuff, there is one thing missing. They have no TV.

I open the book on soybeans I got from the school library. It's really boring. Much as I'd like to get my mind on something else, it immediately goes back to the necklace. Time is ticking by, getting closer to Friday every second. I don't even want to think what Professor Albany will do if I don't have it by then. I can't just sit here. I have to do something.

I wonder if Mrs. Mansard could have taken the necklace. She's always saying she doesn't believe in rules. Maybe that includes taking what belongs to someone else.

I go upstairs to check on Boo. She looks like a little princess asleep in her sleigh bed. Her parents' room is down the hall. I shouldn't really snoop, but under the circumstances I have to take every opportunity that comes along.

Their bedroom is huge. They have some kind of a rug for a bedspread. I open Mrs. Mansard's closet, telling myself I'm not being nosy, just gathering information. I don't know what I expected, but all I find are a lot of colorful clothes and weird shoes.

I check her dresser. She has a collection of old-fashioned perfume bottles in a semi-circle. Feeling kind of nervous, I open her top drawer. I stop for a second and listen. Getting caught once in a day is enough for me. Happily, I hear nothing. My hands and face are starting to feel sweaty.

I wouldn't be doing this if I wasn't really in trouble. The drawer has lots of scarves, and a tray of earrings and necklaces. I look through them quickly. Professor Albany's necklace isn't there. Then I see the box. It's dark wood with an inlaid mother-of-pearl design. It's the kind of box I would keep special stuff in if I had any.

I look for a way to open it, but it seems like it is a solid cube. I give it a couple of shakes and hear something inside, but still can't see how to open it. It must be one of those boxes that have secret panels that make it open, but where?

I think I hear a car pulling up out front. I quickly replace the box and shut the drawer. My heart is thumping as I run to the stairs. I rush down to the living room, expecting to hear the front door open. But it doesn't happen. False alarm.

If the necklace is here, I'm sure it must be in that trick box. I collapse in a chair and let my heartbeat return to normal. Just when I'm starting to feel regular again, I realize I was carrying the soybean book when I went upstairs. And I didn't bring it down with me.

I am sure I hear the Volvo out front now. There is a certain way the brakes squeak. I make a mad dash for the stairs and go up three at a time. I've got to get that book before the Mansards come in. If they see the book in their bedroom, they'll know I was in there and ask a lot of questions I can't answer. I just can't afford to lose another babysitting job.

At full speed, while trying to tip toe, I head for the Mansard's bedroom. Without even slowing down, I reach the room, grab the book and run out. As I get back to the stairs, I hear the key in the front door lock. No time to walk, so I slide down the banisters.

I make it off the second banister as the door begins to open. Two leaps and I'm back in the living room. I fall in the chair and open the book as the door closes and they start up the stairs to the level I'm on.

Trying to appear as relaxed as possible, I look up as they walk into the living room. "Home already?"

Any chance of getting any more information out of Mrs. Mansard is blown when her husband says he'll take me home. Not that she'd be likely to tell me what is in a locked box in her dresser that I shouldn't even know about.

Mr. Mansard asks me about school. The regular sort of conversation adults have with kids my age when they don't know what else to say. I try to think of a way to ask him about Professor Albany. Like maybe he'll tell me what his wife wouldn't. But I can't think of any way to ask him without sounding like I'm nuts.

"Thanks again, Blue, for coming at the last minute. I'm sure my wife will be calling you again." Mr. Mansard waits while I go inside. At least, he didn't make any cracks about my building.

It's late, but I call Yvonne anyway.

"So, do you think Mrs. Mansard took the necklace?" Yvonne sounds like she is lying down.

"I don't know." I have the phone pulled into the closet next to my room. I hear my father pass on his way to the kitchen for his nightly cup of tea.

"Well, what are you going to do?" She sounds worried.

"I don't know." I hate to keep repeating myself, but I can't think of anything else to say.

We hang up, and I sit there for a moment. I can hear the tea kettle start to whistle.

I smell the tea brewing as I come in the kitchen. My father's in his pajamas. He smiles when I come in and takes out another cup.

"Everything all right?" He checks over my face. This is my moment to spill my story. When I hesitate, he asks again.

"Yeah, it's just this stupid soybean report I have to do." I just can't tell him the mess I'm in.

He pours lots of milk and a little sugar in my tea and gives it to me. We sit together, drinking in silence. I think he knows it isn't the soybean report that's bothering me.

Chapter Twelve

You know how they say when it rains it pours? Wednesday that's what my life feels like. First, it's raining on the way to school. And it's not your nice little shower either. It's coming down so hard it feels like the rain drops are being thrown instead of falling. I have my umbrella, but the wind grabs it and breaks its ribs. I'm beyond soaked by the time I get to school—I'm a sponge.

Then Miss Hooper wants a progress report on our food projects right after we do the Pledge of Allegiance. She goes around the room, asking what we've done so far. She likes pretty much everybody's stuff—except mine.

When I show her my notes, she actually holds them up in front of the class. "Blue, I don't know what you're waiting for. The report is due on Friday," she says. The class kind of snickers, and I would like to drop through the floor right then. Just before she moves on to the next kid, she turns back, and sighs like I'm some kind of hopeless case. "And, young lady, I certainly hope you find a way to make your report more interesting than these notes."

I can't exactly explain that I have a few things on my mind, and that last night when I planned to really get going on the report, I ended up snooping around trying to find out if one of my babysitting customers is the real jewel thief. So, I sit there in my squishy-wet shoes and clammy clothes and just take it. The only good thing that happens during the rest of the day is my clothes dry out and at lunch, I see Shane Calavedo reading the poster about the upcoming upper grade social.

"Hey," he says when I go by.

"Hey," I say back to him.

"You think this do is worth going to?" he says, pointing to the poster.

"Everybody goes," I say. "It's in the gym and they have balloons and streamers." Is that the best I can do? Saying they have balloons and streamers? I wish I could think of something better to say, but I have a temporary mind freeze.

Shane nods his head like he's thinking about it, then he looks at me. "Think I'll go. Maybe I'll see you there." When the bell rings he heads back upstairs toward his class.

For a minute, I can't move. Did he really say he would see me there? What if he asks me to dance? The thought makes me feel sort of bubbly inside, like I'm excited and scared at the same time.

Then it's back to bad Wednesday.

"Omigod, that was tough luck about your report," Samantha Parker says with the phoniest sounding sympathy I've ever heard as we leave the building at the end of school.

Yvonne, true-blue friend that she is, catches up and defends me. "Blue's report is going to be brilliant when she finishes it. You'll see," she says to the bunch of kids standing around us.

"Yeah, right." Samantha makes a face and shakes her head, and everyone laughs. "I'll call you later," she says to Yvonne. After the fuss yesterday, she told Yvonne she thought they ought to just divide their report in half and work separately.

Yvonne and I stand there while the rest of our class moves out toward Kimbark Avenue.

"Oh, no, I forgot my key again," Yvonne says, after checking her pockets and school bag. "Want to come to the mummy museum with me?"

"Sure," I say, waiting while she gathers up her stuff. "Are you going for some kind of record? This makes you three for three this week," I say laughing.

Yvonne just rolls her eyes as we go out onto the tree-lined sidewalk. "It's not like I plan it, you know. I thought I picked it up this morning." She gives me one of those hands on her hip looks as we wait for a car to go before we cross the street.

I just wish my problems were as easy to solve. At least, it has stopped raining and the sun's out. But now it feels sticky-hot which is weird for May. It usually doesn't get like this until summer. I am glad for the shady street and even more for the cool inside the Oriental Institute.

"What's all that?" There are piles of boxes next to the gift shop.

"It's because of the show starting Friday." Yvonne points to the sign announcing the Antiquities of Egypt Exhibit.

Mrs. Johnson hears us and comes out from behind the boxes. She smiles and says "hi" to me. Then she turns to Yvonne and shakes her head.

"Forgot your key again?" Mrs. Johnson says. "I told you I thought you ought to wear it around your neck."

Yvonne gives her mother one of those *oh, puleeze* looks, like she would be caught dead with something like little kids wear. "As long as you two are here, how about some help?" Mrs. Johnson points to a pile of different sized boxes. The bigger ones have books, and the smaller ones have trays of jewelry. Yvonne and I put down our school stuff. Mrs. Johnson tells us the books go in the empty case along the wall, and the jewelry belongs in the extra display case that has been added for the show.

"So, do you think Mrs. Mansard's the one? I mean the one who really took the necklace," Yvonne asks as I spread open the top of a box.

"Well, she likes that kind of jewelry," I say, taking out a tray of old-looking bracelets. "Mrs. Mansard would like these."

Just then, Mrs. Johnson walks by. "Do you know Liza Mansard? "

I nod and explain about babysitting for them.

"She's bought a lot of pieces from us, you know. But a lot of her things are the real stuff, not copies like these. She collects antique jewelry." Mrs. Johnson holds up an assortment of earrings, necklaces and bracelets. I gasp and Yvonne gives me a funny look. I feel like I'm going to explode if I don't say something soon, but I can't talk in front of Mrs. Johnson. I have to wait while she places what she's holding in the glass case, and goes back to get more.

"See that necklace," The words burst out. "That's it." I point to the one lying in the middle of the glass case as I move closer. Yvonne gives me a "I don't know what you're talking about" look. I have to take a deep breath so I can explain.

"That's just like the necklace that was stolen from the Albanys'," I whisper, not wanting her mother to hear. But now that I'm closer, I realize it isn't exactly like it. "Well, almost, anyway. It has the same gold-colored beads only they're mixed with red, blue and turquoise ones. And it has teardrop shaped things hanging on it, but they're made out of black stones instead of little pieces of red, blue and turquoise wrapped in gold."

"Wow. So that's what it looks like," Yvonne says, staring at it real hard.

"Almost what it looks like, " I repeat. Meanwhile, my mind is clicking away. "I've got an idea. I wonder how much something like that costs." I lean over and stare at the string of beads and stones.

Yvonne shrugs. "Why?"

"I was thinking—if there's one just like the missing one in the box over there," I say nodding toward it, "Maybe I could take my computer fund and buy it. And then..." This is the part where my plan starts to break down. "Sneak it into the Albanys', and put it someplace where they can find it."

"I'm not helping you with that part." Yvonne jumps up and puts her hands behind her back, like the glass case is suddenly filled with squirming snakes.

"At least let me find out how much it costs." I go over to Mrs. Johnson and ask her the price of the necklace we were looking at. She tells me an amount that would wipe out my computer fund plus all the other money I have. But when I ask her if she has one with all gold colored beads and teardrop shaped charms made out of little pieces of red, blue and turquoise stones, she gives me a funny look. She goes back to the book department and comes back thumbing through one as she walks.

"Is this what you mean, Blue?" She points to a page. It is exactly like the photo Professor Albany showed me.

"Yes," I say excitedly. "Do you have one?'

Mrs. Johnson does a strange thing. She starts to laugh. Then she stops. "If I did, Blue, it would be way more than your price range. Try priceless."

"Could you translate into human language?" Yvonne says, giving her mother a funny look.

Mrs. Johnson shows me the section of the book that talks about the necklace. "Maybe this will explain."

I take it and lean against the wall. The more I read, the gladder I am that I have something to hold me up. The book explains that someone named Sir Edmund Crane had the necklace in his private collection. He had loved Egypt and traveled there often a long time ago when people broke into the tombs and pyramids and stole all the valuable stuff and then sold it to people like Sir Edmund. But when he died, he said he wanted the necklace to go home to Egypt where it belonged. It was supposed to be sent to the Egyptian Museum in Cairo, but it never got there.

"The book kept calling it Nefertiti's necklace. Why does her name sound familiar?" I ask. Then Mrs. Johnson points at this statue of a woman with a big hat right near the entrance.

"That's Nefertiti," she says.

"Oh, that's her," I say. I've passed the statue maybe a million times and never really noticed it until now. Mrs. Johnson says she was married to this Pharaoh named Ahkenaton.

"It was really her necklace?" I say, looking at Mrs. Johnson.

She nods. "Well, thought to be anyway."

"And it was supposed to be in a museum in Egypt?" I ask, repeating what I read.

"But it never made it along with the rest of Sir Edmund's collection."

I swallow hard and trade uncomfortable looks with Yvonne. "Why are you so interested in the necklace? Some school project?"

"No," Yvonne and I say at the same time.

Mrs. Johnson just keeps looking at us, waiting for one of us to say something. I'm in shock. It was bad enough being accused of stealing what I thought was just a regular necklace, but now I find out it's the only one in the world. And it was stolen before it got stolen this time. Like it's double stolen.

I suddenly wonder how Professor Albany got the necklace.

"What do they think happened to the necklace?" I am doing my best to sound just curious.

"It probably ended up on the black market," Yvonne's mother says. "That's what they call the way illicit items are sold," she explains. "It disappeared quite a while ago, so it may have passed through a number of hands. There are whole web sites devoted to lists of missing antiquities. I think it is just terrible how some people want to own things that belong to a country's history." Then she laughed. "Sorry girls, I'll end the lecture."

"If it's really priceless, how would the thief know what to charge?"

"I didn't know you were so interested in Egyptian artifacts," Mrs. Johnson says. "They charge what they can I get, I guess. Whatever it is, I'm sure it's more than your budget allows," she says with a smile. For a moment, I wonder if she knows why I'm asking all the questions, but then I realize she's just joking.

Yvonne and I finish helping and leave. Outside, we walk past two guys with dreadlocks and khaki jackets. The sidewalk is filled with U. of C. students lugging bags of books.

"I guess you ditched the plan to buy a replacement for the necklace," Yvonne says.

"Yeah, you could say that. I can't believe it turned out to be one of those only-one-in-the-world things. I'm back to hopeless."

"What about that Mrs. Mansard? You did hear my mother mention that she collects antique jewelry? Maybe she added something to it," Yvonne says.

"But how am I going to find out? I can't just show up and offer to babysit." I think back to the box I found at the Mansards and wish I could get another chance to find out what's inside.

"Tomorrow's Thursday already. What are you going to do?" Yvonne asks as we keep going down the street.

"Don't you get tired of asking me that?" I answer, moving around a couple walking with their arms around each other.

"I'm just trying to help," she says.

We part at 57th Street. I know Yvonne means well, but every time she asks me what I'm going to do, I realize I haven't got a clue and time is melting. The only thing I know for certain is I have to work on my soybean report. Miss Hooper said she's concerned that I'm "not moving at the same speed on this project as the others in the class are." She said it loud enough for everyone to hear, too. Then she said she wanted to see my work again tomorrow. And she didn't sound like she was just trying to be helpful. Since tomorrow comes ahead of Friday, soybeans have to come ahead of the necklace.

But who would have guessed that while sorting through soybean stuff I'd end up finding out more about the necklace?

Chapter Thirteen

My mother surprises us with a new hamburger dish for dinner. This one she calls Indian curry. It's meat and peas with curry powder mixed in. She serves it over rice. Not that I'm hungry, anyway. I have way too much on my mind. Friday is coming closer and closer every second.

All during dinner, my brother-the-brain just keeps talking about college. Mostly, it's about where he'd like to go. My parents keep looking at each other and shaking their heads. I guess they're all expensive schools.

For once, I'm glad everyone is ignoring me.

After dinner, I look at what I have written down for my report and open the one book on soybeans I have. It's so boring, I almost go to sleep reading it. This just isn't going to work. Unless I come up with something better, my report is going to stink.

I'm trying to think what to do when this idea hits me. I can't use the school library now, but there's 57th Street Books. They're real nice about letting you look around and read before you buy. They even have places to sit.

My parents must still be freaked out about my brother's college thing, because they barely notice when I tell them I'm going to the bookstore.

57th Street Books is real cool. Since it's in the basement of an apartment building, the only view you get from the windows is feet going by—except you can see whole dogs. I go into the second room, the one that has books on food. The trouble is, the only books they have on soybeans are cookbooks. I look through them anyway, hoping I'll find something exciting.

The bookstore is pretty quiet, but I keep noticing people going to the next room. After a while, I get curious and follow a man in a blue sports jacket.

I'm surprised to see rows of chairs and a table in front. Then I see the sign and remember. It's the same sign Yvonne and I noticed on the window advertising the talk Shane's mother is doing about her book. She's off standing in the corner talking to one of the people who works at the bookstore. I check out the chairs for Shane, but he's not there.

Nobody seems to be sitting in the first row, so I take a seat on the end of it. Who knows? Maybe her book has something about soybeans in it.

"Good evening, everyone," the bookstore employee says, standing in front of the table. "I have the honor to introduce tonight's speaker, Sophia Calavedo author of *Cindi and Ahkenaton*. It's part of the Time Travelers' series."

Everyone applauds, and I get the feeling there's not much chance she'll be saying anything about soybeans.

Sophia Calavedo comes up behind the table. Her golden hair, which is the same color as Shane's, is done up in a bun thing. She's wearing the same black dress she had on for the Albanys' party, but she's added a jacket and different jewelry. I bet she's the kind who has one of those mix-and-match wardrobes I always see in magazines. They always show all these outfits you can get out of only a few pieces. You know, you can wear the jacket over the dress, or the skirt or pants. There's usually a shirt that doubles as another jacket and goes with everything, too. And some kind of tank top that you change by what jewelry you add. Today's outfit makes her look much more serious.

"People just seem fascinated with ancient Egypt," Mrs. Calavedo says. She doesn't seem nervous at all talking in front of all those people. If I had to do it, I'd be stumbling over my words and blushing, too. "I decided to take Cindi Rosco and send her to ancient Egypt. What happens when a modern woman goes back to the time of Ahkenaton and Nefertiti?" she says.

I perk up at the name Nefertiti. And I realize, since Shane's mother was at the party, she's a suspect, too.

She begins by talking about what it was like back then. I listen closely now, waiting to see if she says anything about jewelry. She doesn't and pretty soon starts talking about her main character Cindi and what she has to learn before she can come back to the present. That's when I begin to zone out. I come to when she gets to the end and says she'll be taking questions.

This could be the only chance I get to talk to her about Professor Albany's necklace. There's got to be something I can say. I rack my brain while the others in the audience ask her long questions that seem to be mostly about them instead of her book.

She announces she'll be signing copies. I decide that might be a better time to talk to her. A bunch of people get ahead of me in line as she sits down behind the table. There is a pile of books next to her.

I hope this doesn't take too long. It's getting later and later, and I am not doing anything about soybeans.

"Yes?" She says it like it's a question when it's finally my turn, and she notices I'm not holding a book.

"Hi, I'm Blue Schwartz," I say hoping I don't sound too dopey. "I was at the Albanys when they had the party—" Just then, I see Shane come in. He's got on a Hawaiian shirt covered with hula dancers. He nods at his mother, and she waves back. I turn and smile at him.

"Hey," I call nodding.

He says "Hey" back. For a couple seconds, I forget what I'm doing, but then the people behind me in line begin to move around and make impatient noises.

"Are you one of Shane's school mates?" Sophia Calavedo asks. I nod.

"Did you want to ask me something?" she says.

I'm under a lot of pressure here. The people behind me are getting very restless. They're shifting their weight back and forth and breathing kind of loud.

I start off by bringing up the Albanys' party again and repeat I was there too. "Did you see the necklace in the glass case?"

"I certainly did. I'm fascinated with all things connected to that time," she says. "It's certainly a magnificent piece. I mean, to hold something in your hands that Nefertiti might have touched." She stops like the thoughts are just too much for her. Then she goes on. "It would be like reaching across time." Sophia Calavedo keeps looking at me.

"Yeah, I guess it is. But do you remember where it was when you left?"

The people behind me are getting even more restless. I can hear people asking each other what the holdup is.

"Oh, dear, I don't know. I remember handing it to someone. But I don't remember who. You know there was so much commotion with the tray of glasses falling. Audrey thinks someone pushed her," Sophia Calavedo says, shaking her head. She gives me a confused look, as if she's wondering why I'm asking so many questions about it.

I'm hoping to get one more question in. I'm about to ask if Audrey, or Mrs. Albany to me, has any idea who pushed her, but I get hustled by the man in the sports jacket.

"There are others waiting, " he says in a pointed tone while giving me the evil eye.

I say a fast goodbye and move on. Shane is sitting with his elbows resting on his knees. I'm about to say "hey" to him again when I notice Zack Mason. I guess he doesn't have to spend all his time being Professor Albany's teaching assistant. He's sitting in a corner with his nose in a big book with a glossy cover. He doesn't even look up when I go by.

But Shane does. He kind of gives me a wave with his face. I wonder if we'll ever have a real conversation. It's almost dark now, and I hurry down the street. I can't help but wonder if touching the necklace was such a big deal to Sophia Calevedo, owning it might be even better. I don't want it to be her, though. I don't want it to be Mrs. Mansard, either. But most of all, I don't want anyone to think it's me.

I'm in trouble when I get home.

"Where have you been?" My father says when I walk in. He takes out his pocket watch and checks it. He's probably just about the only person in the world who uses one of those instead of a wristwatch. "Blue, it's after eight."

My mother joins him in wanting to know where I was.

"It's nice to know how well everybody listens to me. I told you I was going to the bookstore."

I can see I got them, and they both back off. They completely forget they were angry when I tell them about going to look for stuff on soybeans for a school thing. I go in my room and slump on the bed. I'm not any closer on my school report. Then I remember something. Mrs. Bliss has "National Geographics" from the beginning of time. Maybe I can find something on soybeans in one of those.

My parents don't object when I tell them I'm going to see her.

Like always, Mrs. Bliss seems happy for the company. "Come in, dearie. You missed Chef Randy tonight. Are you all right?"

I tell her about the soybean report and the rest of it, too. About creeping around people's houses and about the suspects so far and how I hope it isn't either one of them.

"Oh, and the necklace turns out to be really old and some guy left it to the Cairo museum, but it got stolen first. And now it's stolen again. I guess that makes it double stolen." I let out my breath when I finish.

"Well, dearie, you've certainly been busy. At least I may be able to help you with your soybean problem." She takes me into her dining room. All the walls have book shelves. One whole area has nothing but old National Geographics.

"My daughter says I should throw them out, but it's so hard." She takes one down and thumbs through it. "Isn't this beautiful?" She holds up a picture of giraffes running. "Now, let me see. It's information on soybeans you want, isn't it?"

Anybody who thinks old people don't have good memories hasn't seen Mrs. Bliss. Out of all those shelves of magazines, she only has to go through a few before she comes up with an article. "You know, dearie, there is something that keeps coming up in my mind. You said the necklace was double stolen." I nod and she continues. "Remember how I said it was strange when that Albany fella didn't call the police after he caught you in his house?"

I nod again.

"Don't you see, that explains it."

I guess my expression makes it pretty clear I don't understand, so she explains it better.

"He wouldn't really want to call the police. They'd start checking on the necklace and probably find out what he was claiming to be his was stolen property. No doubt, they'd start asking him a lot of questions he wouldn't want to answer. When you're dealing with illegal things, you don't want the police involved, Blue. Just suppose some drug dealer gets his stash stolen. He isn't about to report to the police."

I look at Mrs. Bliss in surprise. I didn't know she knew about stuff like that.

"I watch television, too. I know all about rap music and pierced lips and tattoos. My daughter likes to think I live in some old-fashioned land, but I keep up with what's happening. Even the bad stuff."

I'm listening, but something is trying to pop up in my mind. It's the police thing. Why is it ringing a bell?

Chapter Fourteen

"**P**eople think chocolate is just some kind of candy," Walter Jackson says to Miss Hooper when she stops next to his desk. She's going around the room checking how we're doing on our food project reports. "But, you know, those Indian guys that discovered it thought it was some kind of magic drink," he explains. He's supposed to just be talking to her, but we can all hear him.

"Good work, Walter," Miss Hooper says, putting a check mark on his notes.

"Yeah, and you know, billions of people eat some every day," Walter continues. He has one of those annoying voices like a straight line that just keeps on going. "And Miss Hooper, did you know it can cause some people migraine headaches, and one of its better features is that it melts at body temperature. And..."

"Thank you, Walter. That's quite enough. Let's save something for your oral report."

I'm watching Miss Hooper work her way toward me. The sweat is already making me feel clammy. I did find some new stuff in Mrs. Bliss's "National Geographics" and her encyclopedia. I hope my teacher likes my notes.

Denzel Richmond holds up a poster. "I got it from the butcher at the grocery store, Miss Hooper." Even though he's supposedly showing it only to our teacher, everyone can see what it is. People are nudging each other and a lot of people are saying "yuck," but they're still looking at it like they're really interested.

"How clever of you to have gotten this diagram of a cow showing where the different cuts of beef come from, Denzel."

"Yeah, Miss Hooper. That's where they get tongue," Denzel says pointing, "from the actual tongue."

It's making me sick for a lot of reasons. Somehow I never thought about beef really meaning cow. And I never put together that stuff my mother put in sandwiches with something in a cow's mouth until now. I am sure I will never eat it again. And I'm feeling sick because everybody seems to have something interesting going for their report. Or at least Miss Hooper seems to think so. I don't think she's going to like what I have.

Samantha and Yvonne show Miss Hooper all the pictures they've cut out of magazines, while they fire facts at her. Samantha even manages to *not* say "omigod" every two seconds.

"Nobody knows exactly where ice cream came from, but it's been around forever," Samantha says with a confident shake of her head. "In the 1600s, people in Europe mixed ice and snow with fruit and spices. Something called saltpeter helped freeze it."

Miss Hooper nods with approval. Then Yvonne pipes up. "The first ice cream cones were served in the 1904 World's Fair in St. Louis."

"Good, good," Miss Hooper says. "You girls are moving in the right direction. I'm sure your report will be excellent like your other work."

I'm next. My teacher's smile goes away as she picks up my notes.

"Soybeans are really amazing." I put on my brightest voice. "You know they use the oil in all kinds of things like carbon paper and explosives—"

"Blue," Miss Hooper interrupts. "This is a food report. Human food," she says and I know she's looking at the part about how the meal is used in pet food.

"Do you have any other notes?" she says.

I point to the other side of the sheet, and she flips it, glancing over it quickly.

"Soybeans can foster flatulence," she reads out loud in a voice everyone can hear.

Denzel starts laughing. "You know what that means… soybeans make you fart."

The whole class starts laughing too, and Miss Hooper's look is so cold, she could freeze a volcano.

"It isn't all on the paper," I say, trying to save myself. "They're really super food. Even for the ground. The roots of the plant feed the soil. They're called green manure." As the words leave my mouth, I know I have made a mistake.

Denzel starts laughing again. "Gas and manure. Some food report, Schwartz."

I know I am in deep trouble now. Miss Hooper leans over, shaking her head. "Blue, you always make things so difficult for yourself. You pick a bizarre topic and bring in strange information that has nothing to do with the assignment. Why don't you just try following the rules for once?"

There is dead silence in the room. I know everyone is looking at me. My face feels like it's on fire. This day is not going well. Somehow I get through the rest of it, despite Denzel now referring to me as Bean Fart Blue.

Yvonne walks out with me when the final bell rings.

"Got my key," she says holding it out. It's on a neat looking scarab key chain her mother must've gotten her. "Want to come over?" She pats me on the arm. "Maybe I can help you with your report." She lets her voice drop. "And the *other* situation."

"Thanks for reminding me," I say like I am anything but grateful. I was so busy being embarrassed by Miss Hooper, I actually had forgotten about the necklace.

"Blue, it's Thursday," Yvonne says in a frantic whisper. "You didn't find it, did you?"

"Not exactly," I say shrugging. "But there have been some new developments."

"Okay, spill," my friend orders.

I glance around at the groups of kids hanging around the school. "Not here."

"C'mon over then. We can talk at my house," my friend says, starting toward the street, pulling me with her. "We just have to walk Trixie first."

That's the best news I've had all day. I love Yvonne's dog. She's brown and has short hair and a tail like a curlicue and the closest I'm going to get to having a dog. Eric-the-brain is also Eric-the-allergic.

Trixie is by the door when we open it. She is so glad to see us she dances around in circles. When I sit down on the couch, she climbs up next to me and cuddles. That's the thing about dogs, they love you no matter what, even if somebody thinks you're a jewel thief. After I've given her lots of pets and a tummy rub, Yvonne tells her to get her leash. Just like she understands English, Trixie runs off and comes back actually holding it in her mouth.

"Okay, you can spill now," Yvonne says as we walk Trixie down the empty street. She's letting me hold the leash. She's also letting me help clean up after Trixie. I wouldn't mind being left out of that part.

I tell her about Shane's mother and how I talked to her at the book signing. "She acted all excited about touching the necklace. She said it was like reaching through time or something."

"Ooh," Yvonne says. "Maybe she just reached through the glass case."

"I don't want it to be her," I say. "I don't think it would help my chances with Shane if I pointed out his mother's a jewel thief."

"You didn't want it to be that woman you babysit for. And you don't want it to be Shane's mother. Blue, it's Thursday. You better want it to be somebody besides you."

"Thanks for another one of your friendly reminders." I say as we get back inside the apartment. We take Trixie's leash off and all head for the kitchen.

We check out the refrigerator. She's about to close it, saying there's nothing in it, but I stop her.

"Nothing ready, but I could cook something."

Yvonne is impressed and urges me to feel free to go crazy.

"Maybe Professor Albany won't really call the police," I say, taking out some eggs, milk and butter. She shows me where the bread is, and I see the bananas.

"Can I use these?"

"Sure. But why wouldn't he call the police?" she asks. Trixie flops down on the floor in the corner.

I take out a flat bowl and a frying pan as I tell her about what Mrs. Bliss said about him not wanting to because the necklace is double stolen.

"Maybe he won't. But for sure, he'll call your parents."

That sinks in as I crack the eggs and add some milk. Then I mix them by flicking a fork back and forth the way Chef Randy does as I picture my parents hearing I'd stolen something. They'd feel responsible even if they knew I didn't really take it. They'd say they'd replace it. Then they'd find out about the priceless part.

I let the egg mixture sit while I melt some butter in the frying pan. I'm always very careful when I use the stove.

"He wouldn't really call them," I say hopefully.

Yvonne just nods. "I bet he would."

Somehow, I manage to keep making the French toast. When it gets those nice brown marks on each side, I slide the finished product on two plates. Then I add the bananas to the frying pan.

"Oh, yuck. What are you doing?" Yvonne demands as I start to stir the bananas around the pan.

"You'll see. They taste delicious," I say, but Yvonne just shakes her head.

"Chef Randy again, huh?" I nod, and she laughs. "That guy makes some weird stuff."

She goes to get the silverware and stuff. Then she gets out some glasses and a bottle of juice and puts them on the table, while I finish cooking the banana slices. They're all dark and glossy as I pour some on each of the plates and bring them to the table. I slide into my seat.

Yvonne decides to be daring and spears a banana slice. She cringes as she puts it in her mouth. Then when the taste hits her, her whole face lights up.

"Oh, yum. It's like totally different than a regular banana," she says, going back for more.

At least, I can do one thing right. I'm going to ask Yvonne to pass the juice, but she's so into the bananas. So I reach across the table for it, managing to knock over my glass in the process. Before I can make a fast save, it crashes to the floor. Pieces of it splatter all over the place.

"One more thing not going my way today. Sorry," I cry jumping up. "I'll clean it up."

Yvonne gets up to help. "Let me help. I'll get the broom."

It only takes a few minutes to sweep up the mess. But when we get ready to sit down again, her plate is empty.

"Trixie," Yvonne yells. We both look at the same time and see her sitting under the table licking her lips. "I forgot. She has this habit of snatching things off the table when nobody's looking."

I stare at the empty plate. It reminds me of something, but what? Then, like in a flash, something shakes loose in my brain. I jump up and yell, "omigod." Yvonne thinks I'm yelling about her missing French toast and starts telling me we can make more, but I interrupt her.

"It's not about the French toast." I tell her, barely able to contain my excitement. "I can't believe it. I know who has the necklace. And now everything makes sense," I call, running out of the room. Yvonne is right behind me.

"Why don't you call the police or Professor Albany and tell them."

"The police don't even know it's missing and Professor Albany would never believe me. I have to get proof." We are at her front door.

We both look back toward the kitchen just in time to see Trixie running off with the other piece of French toast.

"Trixie," Yvonne screams, throwing up her hands. Then she turns to me. "Do you at least have a plan?"

"Not exactly," I say before I run down the stairs.

"At least tell me who it is," she yells after me.

I don't have time to answer.

Chapter Fifteen

It's already late, almost 5 o'clock. The air feels hot and stuffy outside as I rush toward the campus. The sky is a yellowy-gray that looks downright creepy. Everything is very still, like the wind just stopped completely.

I have to rush around students going the opposite way. Sometimes they take up the whole sidewalk and barely move to let me by. When I get to the campus, I don't know which way to go. Suddenly, all the gray buildings look the same to me. The first building I go into turns out to be wrong. I rush out as secretaries and other people who work there are leaving. I cross the quadrangle and realize the building at the back is the one I want. As soon as I get inside, I rush up the stairs and run down the hall to an office. The door is locked.

I lean against the wall, trying to figure out what to do. Just then, a door opens down the hall. It has Ladies written on it, and I realize it's the bathroom. I run up to the woman who walks out.

I'm desperate now. I forget about being shy or worrying what I'm going to say. I just grab her arm. She kind of gasps.

"Excuse me. I'm looking for someone. It's kind of an emergency."

I guess I must have frightened her, just grabbing her like that. She seems to relax a little when she hears what I want.

"Sure, I know Zack Mason," she says, taking me to her office. She explains she's the department secretary.

'What exactly is the emergency?" she asks as she looks through a spiral book.

"I suppose emergency is the wrong word." I look at my shoes for a minute hoping a good story will pop into my mind. I am really bothered by this lying thing, but I am in too deep to stop now.

"He lost, I mean I found his cell phone," I say, relieved when the story just seems to roll out of my mouth. No way could I tell her I just figured out he's the one who stole the necklace and I need to find him so I can get him to give it back.

"You could just leave it with me. He always stops by in the morning."

"No!" I say it so loudly even I jump. "I have to get it to him now. It's been ringing all over the place since I found it. He might be missing important messages." She seems to think about it a minute and then shrugs.

"Okay, then." She reaches for the phone. "I'll just call him and you can talk to him about the cell phone."

Uh oh, just when it seemed like things were going well. Why couldn't she have just given me his phone number so I could call him in private. No way am I going to say anything about the necklace with her standing there. The phone begins to ring, and she hands the receiver to me. I avoid looking at her, praying that he isn't home. Maybe then she'll just give me the number.

"No answer," I say handing the receiver back to her, but the ringing is suddenly replaced by a voice saying "hello." The secretary gestures for me to take back the phone. For a moment, we both stand there looking at each other while this funny sounding voice keeps saying "hello." I've gotten myself into it this time. She shakes her head and takes the phone. She explains who she is, and what I'm claiming to have. I am edging my way toward the door when she says something that makes me stop. "Oh, but you sound just like Zack. " She hands me the phone explaining it's his roommate. "See if you can make some arrangements with him for the cell phone."

She picks up her purse and umbrella, sure signs she wants to leave. I stumble around on the phone saying I found Zack's cell. The roommate seems to buy the story. Thank heavens, nobody has asked me how I know the supposed phone belongs to Zack. He says I can drop it off if I want to, and he gives the address. The secretary looks very happy when I finally leave.

Having Zack's address gives me a new idea. What if I could figure a way to look around his place. It would be better than talking to him.

I mean, no way would he just say he took the necklace if I asked him. What was I thinking of? Maybe things are turning around.

Zack's building is near 55th, and all the way there, I try to come up with some kind of plan to find out about the necklace. My story about the phone was so convincing, I have completely forgotten I made it all up.

The building is a little rundown. The front hall looks like it needs a paint job, but it has a buzz door. Zack's roommate must have been standing next to the buzzer, because I barely ring the bell when it goes off. I have to run to get in before it stops. Inside, I pass a few strollers and a bicycle missing its front wheel. The hall smells like someone is cooking lamb chops. When I get to the second floor, a guy with a plaid shirt is standing in the doorway. He's got the same kind of messed up looking hair as Zack, only his is kind of dark blonde.

"So, you got the cell?" he says, holding out his hand.

"The...?" What a time to remember the truth. He's looking at me, and I'm looking at him, all the while trying to figure out what to do.

"Are you going to hand it over?" he says, pushing his hand toward me again.

I get an idea. "I'll just put it in Zack's room, if you don't mind. Where is it?"

My heartbeat picks up, as he shrugs and shows me the way. Zack's room turns out to be at the back of the apartment. The roommate stands in the doorway, and I rush in. I look around quickly as I head toward the desk.

"Nice computer," I say, stopping in front of it. Colorful fish are swimming across the screen. While pretending to admire the screen saver, I am actually checking out the room with the corners of my eyes. Zach's not much of a housekeeper. I take in the unmade bed and a pile of dirty laundry. There's an armchair that probably used to be a nice color. Now, it's kind of faded gray. It's next to a tall dresser which I can't quite see the top of. As an excuse to move closer, I act like I'm admiring the stuff on the walls.

"Nice pictures," I say, pretending to be very interested in the framed photos of downtown Chicago, while I examine the dresser top. No necklace there or anywhere. I suppose it was stupid to think it would be someplace where I could see it. If only I could open a few drawers.

The roommate keeps standing behind me.

"Why don't you just put it on his desk," the guy says, getting impatient.

"Huh? Put what on the desk?"

"The phone. Remember? The thing you found."

"Oh, yeah," I say, as the reason I'm supposed to be there comes back to me. I also remember I don't have it and I better think of something fast. I fumble around in my school bag like I'm looking for it. It is really a little creepy what a good liar I've become.

"Oh, no I must have dropped it on the way over." I give him my best mouth-open, bug-eyed horrified look. As I back out of the room and head for the door, I tell him I'm going to retrace my steps.

He shakes his head and shoves a piece of paper at me. "Here's the number. Give Zack a call when you find it."

I'm barely out the door when he shuts it. I bet that necklace is in there somewhere. If only he'd left me in Zack's room alone for a few minutes, I could have found it.

This is too close to give up. When I get outside, I go around to the back of the building. When I was in Zack's room, I noticed the window looked out on the back porch. Maybe I can get another peek in from outside. Of course, I'll need x-ray eyes to see in those drawers.

I slip through the backyard and head for the wooden stairs that lead up the back of the building. There's nobody around, so

I just go up to the second floor. They have nice big back porches. The kind you can put a table on, if you don't mind eating next to garbage cans.

I crouch down and look in the window. The same stuff is still there, and no necklace has magically appeared. That's when I hear a noise at the back door. I rush to the porch across the way. The roommate opens the inside door and then the security door. He comes out trying to carry a big green trash bag. It must have a week's worth of garbage. It's so full, he doesn't seem to be able to see over the top of it, and he trips coming out the door. The monster bag falls out of his arms. His back is to the door, and he's too busy to notice what's behind him.

I have only a second to think. This is my one chance. While he drags the trash bag to the can, and fights with it to get it in, I make my move. Before he finishes and turns around, I'm in. And by the time he closes the door, I'm already back in Zack's room.

My heart is definitely pounding by now, and my stomach doesn't feel too good, either. Is this breaking and entering or maybe just entering? I slip under the desk and wait. Footsteps go by. The roommate's on the phone, saying he'll meet somebody in five minutes. There's a swish of a nylon jacket, then finally a door opens and closes. Then silence except for the sound of the bubbles on the computer's screen saver.

I come out from under the desk and check its drawers quickly. There's just the stuff you'd expect like pencils with broken lead, and lots of loose paper clips. There's nothing even close to a necklace. The dresser drawers just have socks and stuff. The closest thing to jewelry is one cuff link. I'm still sure the necklace is here somewhere. It's the where that's got me stumped.

I take another look around the room. He'd want to put it someplace nobody would find it, right? All the places I checked were the obvious ones. Where wouldn't you expect to find it? I take a step away. I'm almost at the wall. What if I'm wrong? What if Zack didn't take the necklace? I take another step and since I don't have eyes in the back of my head, I smack into one of the pictures on the wall making it go all crooked. As I try to straighten it, there's a funny noise, like something's scraping the wall. I pull out the picture and look behind. Then I gasp. Carefully, I lift the picture off the nail. A long yellow cord is holding a drawstring bag on the nail. I unhook the cord and open the bag quickly.

The necklace is coiled up like a jewel snake. I just stare at it in amazement for a couple seconds.

Saved. I'm saved.

I put it in my bag and replace the picture. All I have to do now is get the necklace back to Professor Albany. I take a minute to kind of let it all sink in and lean against the desk. I guess I must have pushed the mouse because the screen saver goes off and the sign-on screen for his Internet service shows up.

It must be nice to be hooked up to the Internet. You could spend all the time you want looking up anything, any time of the day or night. You could look up soybeans in the middle of the night, or right now.

I should really get out of here while the coast is clear. I listen for a minute, and there's just quiet. I don't even sit down. I just click on sign-on.

I go to the Web and type in soybeans and click on search. It takes a few moments and then a screen of possibilities shows up, only none of them have anything to do with what I'm looking for. I check the search box and see I typed in roymean by mistake. I'm so busy trying to type it in right I have forgotten where I am, and why I should be concerned when a door opens and footsteps start down the hall. It isn't until a voice yells "What are you doing here?" and I look up and see Zack that I realize I have made it into the big time of trouble.

Chapter Sixteen

Now I know what Goldilocks must have felt like when the bears showed up. Only it was easier for her. She just had to say she was hungry and tired. I have a much harder time coming up with an explanation when Zack wants to know what I'm doing in his room.

And suddenly I'm scared. What if he tries to hurt me? I crouch ready to make a run for it. I guess my face gives away how scared I am.

"Relax, kid, I'm totally non-violent," Zack says, putting up his hands. "Just tell me what you're doing in my room."

I am completely out of stories, so I tell him the truth.

"I figured out you stole the necklace, and I wanted to find it so I could get it back to Professor Albany and get myself out of trouble."

He shakes his head and puts his head in his hands. "How did you know it was me?"

I start to tell him the whole story about Trixie snatching the French toast, but he's not getting the connection.

"I figured out the necklace disappeared during that whole commotion over the broken glasses," I say, getting up. "Just like Trixie got the French toast while we were cleaning up the glass. Except for one thing. Trixie didn't plan it, but you did. Somebody said Mrs. Albany thought she'd been pushed and that's why she dropped the tray." I look him right in the eye. "And then I remembered that you were looking for the broom before there was anything to sweep up, like you knew there was going to be broken glass because you were going to make it happen. And then I guess while everybody was rushing around and you were supposedly going for the broom, you got the necklace."

Zack hits his head with his hand. "And I thought this was going to be so easy."

I look toward the door, wondering if I should try and make a run for it.

Zack starts talking to me like I'm a kid. He must have some short memory. He isn't *that* much older than me.

"You don't understand. I didn't take it because I wanted it. Professor Albany bought a stolen necklace. It's an antiquity. I don't suppose you even know what that means." He shakes his head and his shoulder sag like he's melting. "It means it's a relic of an ancient time. It should be in a museum in the country it's from. I just wanted to get it back where it belongs." He throws me an exasperated look. "Oh, you probably can't understand."

"I understand all right, but you got me in all kinds of trouble, you know." I'm not scared any more, just mad.

He looks like he feels bad. "Sorry."

Then he tells me a whole long story about how he looked up to Professor Albany and thought he was the greatest guy around until he found out about the necklace.

"Man, did that make him tumble off the pedestal I'd put him on," Zack says with a sigh. "I was so angry when I found out the whole story behind the necklace. It's part of Egypt's history and should be where everybody who wants to can see it."

"So then, I guess you were expecting a lot of foot traffic in your room." I point to the picture the necklace was hanging behind. Zack just shakes his head like he thinks I'm some kind of idiot kid again.

"I was never planning to keep it."

"Great, but what about me? Don't you get it? You got me in all kinds of trouble."

"I said I was sorry," Zack says like he means it. "And, if you remember that day at the store, I did tell you the Professor would never really go to the police. There's no way he'd want to disclose that he owned a stolen antiquity. And if the big wheels at the University found out, well, it would disintegrate his reputation."

"Okay, you did tell me about the police thing. I thought you were just being nice, but now I realize you were counting on it for yourself," I say, realizing that it is the not-calling-the-police-thing I couldn't quite remember at Mrs. Bliss's.

He holds out his hand. "So, why don't you just give it back to me."

I don't make a move toward my bag. "What are you going to do with it?"

Zack rolls his eyes. "Like I said, I wasn't ever planning to keep it. I just ran into a problem returning it without getting into trouble myself."

"Can't you just call up the Cairo museum and tell them you have it?"

Zack sort of laughs. "It would be kind of sticky explaining how I got it." His laugh fades into a tired sigh. "I'm beginning to think trying to straighten things out was all a big mistake. I got you in trouble. I've...well at the moment, *you've* got a stolen antiquity. It's just that at that party, I got the sudden impulse to take it and make things right. So, I planned Mrs. Albany's accident with the tray."

All the time he's talking, I'm thinking. When he finally takes a breath, I tell him I think I have an answer.

"C'mon, you're just a kid," he says, shaking his head.

"I'm thirteen, and besides this could work." My mouth slips into a grin as I explain my plan.

I guess Zack starts to believe me, because his face brightens, and he kind of perks up like he isn't melting anymore. He even lets me finish doing my soybean work on his computer. I find a little stuff, like soybeans are the Cinderella of foods, but I'm still looking for that sizzle.

Zack wants the necklace back, but I convince him for the plan to work, I have to keep it.

And then I get this icky feeling. After telling Professor Albany again and again that I don't have the necklace, and don't know where it is, I realize both are no longer true.

My plan has to work, or boy, am I in trouble over my head.

Chapter Seventeen

"You're awfully quiet tonight," my father says at dinner. "Is something wrong?"

I shake my head and push the food around on my plate. No way can I tell them what's going on.

"I thought you liked my spaghetti Italiano," my mother says. I can feel her eyes on me.

"I just not very hungry." I just want to get finished so I can call Yvonne. There is no way this plan will work without her help. All I have to do is talk her into it.

My brother-the-brain keeps looking at me during dinner. I figure he probably likes the new me, all quiet all the time. My father leaves to make a phone call, which means I can't run off and call Yvonne. My mother goes down the hall to the kitchen to whip some cream for the strawberries we're having for dessert.

Eric keeps looking at me now that it is just the two of us at the table.

"How come you're not talking?" he asks. I'm expecting him to say something after that like it's a nice change or something, but instead he says, "Something's wrong, isn't it? You're never this quiet. You need some help with math?"

"Huh? Did you just offer to help me?" I say totally shocked.

"You don't have to act so surprised. Don't you remember how I used to walk you home from school when you were little?" he says.

For a few seconds I think about telling him what's going on, but then I decide not to. I thank him for offering to help, but say I'm not having a problem with math right now. I think that's the end of it, but then he starts telling me about his problems.

He says he's worried about his grades and he's worried about getting into the college he wants and he's worried about getting a big enough scholarship because he won't be able to go to college without it. On top of all of it, he's worried about letting our parents down.

"That's why I study all the time," he says with a little sadness in his voice. "I wish I had more time to play basketball."

Wow. Who knew it was so difficult being the great brain hope of the family? Now I'm glad I didn't tell him about the necklace. He has enough to worry about already.

Eric is about to say something else, but stops when my mother walks in with a glass bowl of cut up strawberries covered with whipped cream.

As soon as I help clear up the dishes, I grab the phone and pull it into the closet. My parents and Eric are outside the door all saying they have to use the phone. Great, now on top of everything else, I have to hurry. I promise I'll be quick, and thankfully they don't stand outside the door waiting.

"I have to talk fast," I tell Yvonne as soon as I get her on the phone.

When I get to the part about having the necklace, she starts to squeal.

"Omigod, Blue, you don't really have it? Omigod, are you crazy?" Then she just says a bunch of "omigods" by themselves. "If you say omigod one more time, I'm going to scream," I say when she stops to breathe. "You have been spending way too much time with Samantha Parker."

"Oh, mi..." Yvonne stops herself. "Oh, no, Blue you're right. Sorry."

"I need your help," I say. I can hear footsteps coming down the hall. Any second somebody is going to say I've been on the phone long enough. I start to talk faster. "I just need you to help me get into that new exhibit at the Oriental Institute."

She laughs and says no big deal, that anybody can get in, but then I tell the tricky part. I have to get in before it opens to the public.

"I don't know, Blue. We could get in a lot of trouble."

"I'm already there," I remind her. "Please."

The banging on the closet door starts. It's Eric-the-brain saying he has to call somebody about his homework. A second later, my father is there too, telling me Eric has to make an important call. Like mine isn't? Of course, they don't know how important.

I say a few more pleases and Yvonne agrees, and we make up a plan. Just as I'm saying good bye, Eric opens the door, looking frantic. I'm sitting on the floor crunched between shoes and boxes. I hang up quickly and hand him the phone.

I feel a little better now that the plan is progressing. Then it comes back to me that our food reports are due tomorrow. No way can I finish mine, especially since I still haven't found anything spectacular to put it in it.

That night, I have trouble sleeping. What if the plan doesn't work? What's going to happen when Miss Hooper calls on me? I get up a couple of times to check my school bag to make sure the necklace is still there. It's hard to believe my whole future depends on that little bit of gold and pretty stones.

Somehow, I get myself to school in the morning. Everybody comes into class carrying charts and folders with neat looking computer labels. Yvonne and Samantha Parker carry in a papier-mâché ice cream cone, so big it takes both of them to hold it. Yvonne looks my way. She mouths omigod, and I laugh.

It's my last smile for a while.

The whole morning is spent on the reports. Each time Miss Hooper calls on somebody, it's getting closer to my turn. I dread being called on. I avoid dealing with it by thinking about what is going to happen after school and the fact that the necklace is sitting in my school bag under my chair. Yvonne is pretty sure her mother will let us look around the exhibit before the big opening tonight. I have already written a note I plan to leave with the necklace. Not exactly written. I cut the words out of magazines like people do for ransom notes so they can't trace the handwriting.

When Miss Hooper finally does call on me, I don't even hear at first.

"Blue—we're waiting," she says sharply.

"Huh?" I look up still thinking about Nefertiti and Egypt and museum exhibits.

By now, everybody is staring.

"Hey, Bean Fart Blue, time for your report," Denzel calls. The whole class laughs. Except, of course, for Miss Hooper.

"That will be enough, Denzel," she says in a threatening voice. Then she turns her attention back to me. Her eyes rest on the empty top of my desk. Her expression gets even darker. I don't have to be a mind reader to know that she's wondering why there aren't any papers or Styrofoam soybeans on my desk.

"Well, Blue..."

"Ah, due to unavoidable circumstances," I begin, trying to keep my voice from shaking, "I don't have my report." At least, it's the truth. Of course, missing a few details.

"Oh, what is it?" She sounds impatient. "Are you going to tell me your dog ate your report?" The class laughs, but Miss Hooper isn't smiling.

"No. I don't even have a dog." I am fighting to keep my voice from quavering. "It isn't like that. I can't exactly explain, but I just couldn't finish it for today." I take a deep breath. "Could I have until Monday?"

Miss Hooper makes a face like I just offered her a snail soufflé. "Miss Schwartz, you are never going to amount to anything if you can't do your work on time." She pauses and then kind of sighs. "You can give your report on Monday— but you'll automatically lose one grade. And if the report is anything like those notes, I'd say you were in danger of a failing mark."

I say "thank you," though I don't know for what.

As soon as school ends, I rush outside and wait for Yvonne. She has to help Samantha Parker carry the papier-mâché ice cream cone to her mother's SUV. Miss Hooper loved the cone and gave them a nice A–.

"C'mon," I say as soon as she joins me. As we head out to the street, I hold my school bag extra tight against me due to its valuable cargo. Everybody else is in their thank-heavens-it's-Friday mood, but me. My stomach feels like it's full of rocks on top of being tied in a knot.

We don't talk on the way to the Oriental Institute. As soon as we get inside, Yvonne runs up to her mother.

"Forgot your key again?" Mrs. Johnson says. She's extra dressed up today in a dark suit and heels. Her blond hair is done up in some kind of twist.

"Yes, I did, mother," Yvonne says stiffly. It seems really obvious she isn't telling the truth, but I guess her mother is so busy with the opening, she doesn't notice. Mrs. Johnson starts to hand her the key.

"As long as we're here," Yvonne continues stiffly, using the speech I gave her, "why don't Blue and I have a look at the new exhibit?"

Mrs. Johnson smiles and smoothes her hand over Yvonne's wiry dark hair. "Sorry girls, no one is allowed in until the opening."

"Are you sure? I mean, Blue was really looking forward to getting to see it." Yvonne gives her mother a pleading look.

"Rules are rules. The head of the museum said nobody in there until tonight. I'll get you in over the weekend, Blue. I didn't know you were such an ancient Egypt fan."

I smile weakly. My plan has just gone down the drain. Yvonne comes over and puts her arm around me.

"Sorry."

"Me, too. What am I going to do?" I look down at my school bag. It's like I have x-ray eyes and can see the necklace. I have to get rid of it.

Mrs. Johnson is busy with a table being set up in the entrance of the museum. I look over at the door to the exhibit hall. The curtains are off and you can see in. I wonder if I might be able to just sneak in. I only need a few minutes to drop off the necklace.

Nobody is watching. I tell Yvonne what I'm going to do. She puts her hand over her ear.

"I can't hear you. I don't want to hear you. I don't know what you're going to do." I'm just going to go and talk to my mother for a few minutes."

Yvonne goes over to her mother and gets her to turn away from me and the door. The people setting up the table aren't paying any attention to me, either.

I take one step backward at a time, slowly moving toward the big glass door. I have my school bag behind me. I take a giant step and almost lose my balance. Yvonne is doing a good job of keeping her mother facing the other way.

My heart is beating so fast, I can feel it in my ears. Just a few more backward steps and I'm there. I ease across the door. Mrs. Johnson starts to turn. I freeze. Yvonne gets her to turn back. One more step. My hand is on the door. I pull. It doesn't move. It's locked. And I'm back at square one.

I walk over to Yvonne and whisper that I couldn't get in.

"I can't hear you," she says, moving away from her mother. "Remember, I didn't hear what you were trying to do. I don't know anything about it."

"You don't have to worry," I say, letting my shoulders slump. "It didn't work." I explain about the door being locked.

"What are you going to do?" she says.

I am about to tell her I'm out of ideas, when suddenly the glass door opens. The very door I was just trying to sneak through. A tall man in a tweed suit walks out.

"Mrs. Johnson," he calls, walking toward Yvonne's mother. "Call maintenance please. We have a flickering light in here."

"Certainly, Dr. Guterfeld," she says, going to the phone. I feel a surge of hope. "This could be my lucky break," I tell Yvonne who answers by going into her not-hearing-what-I'm-saying-or-wanting-to-know-what-I'm-planning-to-do mode. I ease over by the glass door and wait. In a few minutes, a man in a blue shirt with his name on it comes in carrying a ladder and some tools.

"I cut the power to the whole exhibit," the maintenance man says to Dr. Guterfeld as he flips on his flashlight.

Dr. Guterfeld unlocks the door and goes in first. The man with the ladder follows. Just as the last of the ladder goes through the door, I slip in with it.

I stop in the first room and watch the bobbing light from the flashlight as Dr. Guterfeld leads the maintenance man back through the big rooms of the exhibit hall. Their footsteps grow fainter. I steal a look back at the glass door. Yvonne is distracting her mother again. She sees me and winks. I give her a thumbs up.

Okay, I finally managed to get in here. Now, I just need to find a place to leave the necklace where someone like Dr. Guterfeld will find it. Then, I have to get out before they do.

The windows have been covered up, so it's dark in the room I'm in, but not completely thanks to those emergency lights that come on when the power is off. As my eyes get used to the low light, I check out the area quickly. Tall glass cases line the wall. No way is there any place to leave the necklace on one of them. There are some big statues in the corners making creepy shadows.

Then I think I see something ahead that could work.

I keep my ears open to what is going on with Dr. Guterfeld and the man fixing the light. I can't hear everything they're saying, but enough words to figure out what they're doing. It sounds like they're going to be busy for a while.

I creep forward into the next room. In the darkness, I can just make out the outline of some big mummy cases against the wall. Right in the middle of the room is exactly what I'm looking for. It's shaped kind of like a table and has a big top. I open my backpack and take out the necklace and the note.

This is it. All I have to do is lay it on the display case.

I'm careful as I put it down. I don't want it to make some jingle sound as it touches the glass. I put the note next to it, explaining what it is.

Now, all I have to do is get out of here.

And that's when the trouble starts.

The maintenance man says he needs a different screwdriver. Dr. Guterfeld says they better hurry and get it. I hear their footsteps coming toward me. In seconds, they will be where I am. What if they see the necklace or worse, see me? I have to hide, but where? I look around frantically and see the mummy cases against the wall. No way am I going in one of those.

I stick my foot under the case the necklace is on and realize it doesn't go all the way to the floor. It's got legs and thankfully, room for me between them.

I slide under just in time. The circle of light from their flashlights passes right by me.

Oh, no, what if they shine the light on the top of the case and see the necklace?

I hold my breath. My heart is beating so loud, I'm surprised they don't hear it.

Chapter Eighteen

I let out my breath when they keep walking. They didn't see the necklace. I slip to the edge of the display case and peek out just after Dr. Guterfeld and the maintenance man go by. I'm hoping I can slip out while they're getting the tool. But Dr. Guterfeld stands guarding the door while the other guy goes for the screwdriver.

I'm stuck. I move back under the display case, and wait. Meanwhile, my mind starts going crazy with thoughts like what if I can't figure a way to get out of here.

The sound of the door opening interrupts my worrying. Then I hear them walking and talking.

"Can you hurry, please? The exhibit is scheduled to open in about an hour," Dr. Guterfeld says to the maintenance man as I watch two pairs of legs go by toward the back of the exhibit. As soon as I'm pretty sure they're back working on the light, I decide to make my move.

I take a deep breath and come out from under the display case, and start backing toward the door. Big mistake. I bump into a mummy case and jump and almost scream. I change direction and keep swiveling my head around, to see if anyone is coming, and if I am going to bang into something else. So far the coast seems clear. When I get close to the glass door, I look out into the lobby. Problem. Yvonne sees me and starts frantically pointing toward her mother. Her mother is facing the other way, so I don't get what has Yvonne going so crazy. I give her a look like I don't understand and make a move toward the door. Yvonne shakes her head really hard and waves me back. Her mother turns toward her and Yvonne quickly changes the move to acting like there is lint all over her. I see why she was doing it.

Mrs. Johnson steps toward the glass door. I pull out of sight just in time. Two men put down a bunch of poles with red velvet rope between them leading up to the door. It takes them a few minutes to arrange them. I wish they would hurry. When they finally set the whole thing up and leave, Mrs. Johnson walks over to a table being set up in front of the gift shop. I wait until she is busy unfolding a white table cloth.

Yvonne waves madly for me to come.

I grab the door handle, knowing freedom is inches away now. The door doesn't move. I feel for some knob to turn to unlock it, but there isn't one. All I feel is a place for a key, and I bet anything it's in Dr. Guterfeld's pocket. I am locked in. "Omigod," I say to myself not caring if I sound like Samantha Parker. My goose is cooked. I am on my way to jail. They will find me, they will see the necklace, and if I explain how I got it— Well, anyway you look at it, it's bad for me.

I feel all panicky, but remember how Mrs. Bliss said the best thing to do in situations like this is to take a couple of really deep breaths. She said it helps you think straight. I do the deep breathing thing, and I do feel a tiny bit better, but not much. I can see Yvonne, and she looks like she's going to faint.

I feel just terrible. I didn't want to get her in trouble. I slide down and sit against the wall in the shadows, and do the only thing I can do now—wait for Dr. Guterfeld to leave with the maintenance man. This is the worst—just waiting for trouble to find me.

Finally, I hear the ladder banging against itself, and footsteps and voices. I can't help myself. I say "omigod" again. They're getting closer. They're passing through the room with the necklace sitting on the display case. They keep coming, their footsteps getting louder and louder. My heart is pounding.

They come in the room where I am, and head toward the door. Just before they reach it, I start to stand to throw myself at their mercy. But then a miracle happens. I realize they are so busy looking forward in the semi darkness, they don't see me. And I realize I can escape the way I came in.

Maybe.

While Dr. Guterfeld unlocks the door with a key, I scoot against the outside of the ladder. I hear the whoosh of the door opening. I keep my eyes on the ladder and move with it, hoping no one will notice a pair of legs walking below it. As soon as I pass into the lighted lobby, my breath comes out in a gush. I didn't even realize I was holding it.

I'm out. I did it. I made it.

I flatten myself against the lobby wall and just breathe. Dr. Guterfeld and the maintenance man keep going.

"You made it," Yvonne says, oozing relief as she rushes over to me. "Here's Blue," she calls in a totally different voice to her mother. "She just went downstairs to the bathroom."

Mrs. Johnson glances toward me and nods absently, then goes back to all the preparations going on for the opening.

"Let's get out of here," Yvonne says pulling my hand.

I'm glad for the support, my knees still feel kind of weak.

I have never been so glad to be outside. Everything looks wonderful. The big lawn on the campus across the street. All the students crossing kitty-corner. I'm out. I'm free, and I don't have the necklace anymore, and it's where somebody will find it and take it back where it belongs. Case closed. Well, not exactly.

There's still the problem with Professor Albany.

Chapter Nineteen

I have an hour before step two of the plan, so Yvonne and I walk through the campus to Botany Pond. I'm still recovering from the first part. We walk on the little gray cement bridge and sit down.

"I could go with you," Yvonne says, as we lean over the side, looking at our reflections in the only non-lily pad covered part of the water.

I watch the reflection of my head shake in the water. "Thanks, but I don't want to get you in trouble if it doesn't work out."

We just sit there waiting after that. When an hour has gone by, we get up. She hugs me and wishes me good luck, and we go our separate ways.

Zack is supposed to have made sure Professor Albany is in his office.

As I walk across the campus, my mouth gets dry and it's hard to swallow. I go to the building that has Professor Albany's office. As I go up the stairs, I start getting nervous all over again. It feels like my stomach is missing.

I open the door. There's no secretary, just Zack. He gives me a secret thumbs up as I walk in, and then pretends like he doesn't know me.

"Blue?" Professor Albany sounds surprised when he see me. "What are you...?" Then his eyes light up. "It's about the necklace, isn't it. Good idea, young lady, to come to me instead of waiting for me to come after you." He walks out from behind the desk, and I swallow real hard.

"Where is it?" he says gruffly, holding out his hand.

"I, ah, don't exactly have it on me. But I can take you to it."

He grabs my arm. "You little scoundrel. I knew you had it all along." His mouth is set in a straight line and his eyes look mean. He gets impatient and more angry. "I don't know why you didn't just bring it here."

I shrug.

"Okay, then let's go." He moves toward the door, still holding onto my arm. I notice Zack is gone.

"Well, which way?" Professor Albany says when we get outside. Zack and I decided it was best not to tell him where I'm taking him, so I just start walking through the campus and Professor Albany follows.

And not silently either. All the way he keeps saying he knew I was a thief. That old buildings like mine are just filled with kids like me who don't know right from wrong. How good it will be for the neighborhood when all the old slums are torn down. He is so busy talking at me, he doesn't pay too much attention to where we're going.

I lead him up the steps of the Oriental Institute and into the lobby before he looks around with a confused look.

"What are we doing here?" He says it loud and mean, and then seems to realize all the people standing around can hear him, and he says it again, softer.

I don't answer. Meanwhile, he sees a lot of people he knows and they all smile and say hello. It's creepy to see how he can look so friendly toward them, and then get that mean mouth when he looks back toward me.

"What's going on?" he says to me, pulling my arm closer.

Before I can not answer again, Dr. Guterfeld steps through the glass doors I escaped through just a little while earlier. He seems very excited and shakes a man's hand and then brings him into the exhibit.

I take Professor Albany through the red velvet ropes and through the door. There's a big crowd and we are kind of pushed forward with them. It's a lot easier to see now that the lights are on.

Professor Albany is really annoyed. "Blue, what's going on?" he says loud enough that several people look at him.

Dr. Guterfeld is in the second room surrounded by a group of people. "We are all very excited about a mysterious surprise," he says to the group around him.

"Where is my necklace?" Professor Albany says as I keep going toward that second room.

"I'll show you in a second," I say innocently. He doesn't notice that I say show you instead of give you. "Look, there are the Channel 5 people," I say, pointing to a man with a microphone along with another with a camera.

As soon as we get in the second room, I check the top of the display case. It's empty. Then I look inside the case and smile. Finally, something has gone right.

"I want the necklace now," Professor Albany says, pinching my arm.

"No problem," I say and point. There in the glass case on a piece of blue velvet is the necklace.

"What's my necklace doing here?" he sputters. Dr. Guterfeld looks at him

"Your necklace?" Dr. Guterfeld repeats.

All of a sudden, Professor Albany looks a little green. Everyone is looking at him. The news guys have their camera and microphone pointed toward him.

Professor Albany gives me a horrible look.

Then Dr. Guterfeld takes out my note. " Someone left it here this afternoon along with this note. Of course, we still have to authenticate the piece, but I've seen enough pictures to recognize Nefertiti's necklace when I see it. This is an important moment. For any of you who aren't familiar with the story, the necklace belonged to Sir Edmund Crane. It is believed he bought it from some tomb robbers during one of his frequent trips to Egypt. When he died, he left it to the Egyptian Museum in Cairo, which is where it should have been all along, but then I've never made a secret about what I think of those people who try to own pieces of history. On its way to the museum, the necklace disappeared. All we had until now were pictures of it from Sir Edmund's collection."

"And you say this piece is yours?" the museum head says, peering at Professor Albany strangely. "And just what exactly would you be doing with a stolen antiquity? And don't insult my intelligence by telling me you didn't know it was stolen."

Meanwhile the Channel 5 guys are getting it all on tape.

It makes me feel good to see Professor Albany on the hot seat for a change. I move away from him. Mrs. Johnson is standing by the wall. She gives me a funny look as I go by.

Zack comes out from the shadows. For the first time, I notice he looks different. I think he must have used a comb instead of the wind to fix his hair. His eyes are almost dancing.

I go past him, trying to talk without moving my lips. "Mission accomplished."

"Good job," he whispers out of the side of his mouth like we're spies. He doesn't want anyone to know he's involved with the necklace. Zack's afraid he could lose his scholarship or get kicked out of school. I steal a quick glance at him. He's fighting a smile. I feel my lips going up, too. Suddenly, I want to jump around and dance and yell "we did it." But all we do is slip each other a secret high five and go back to acting like we don't know each other.

I just want to get out of there now. It's still sinking in that I did it. That I'm off the hook, that Professor Albany won't be threatening me any more. And I did a good thing. Even though it took a really long way to get there, Nefertiti's necklace is finally going to be where it belongs.

Just then Sophia Calavedo and Shane come in. He's wearing a sports jacket over his Hawaiian shirt.

"Hey, what's up?" he says as I pass.

"Too much to tell," I say as I rush toward the door taking just one little look back.

I wonder how my babysitter boss likes being the one in trouble.

Chapter Twenty

I'm on the news that night. Well, sort of, anyway. Channel 5 does a report about the mysterious return of a valuable antiquity. They have film and everything.

"Is it really Nefertiti's necklace?" the reporter asks pointing the microphone toward Dr. Guterfeld.

"Sir Edmund always called it that," the museum head begins. "But truly, we don't know for sure. As you may know, what happened to Nefertiti after her short term as Ahkenaton's main wife is a bit of a mystery. The best I can say is that it could have belonged to her."

"I understand you just found the piece of jewelry lying there. Any ideas of how it got to the museum?" the reporter asks.

Dr. Guterfeld turns and stares right at Professor Albany. "Not yet, but I certainly intend to get to the bottom of it before I personally make sure it gets to the Egyptian Museum in Cairo."

Professor Albany looks like he wishes he could disappear. I guess I can count them out as babysitting customers.

They replay the news story Saturday morning and Eric sees it. My brother gives me a funny look and asks if I know anything about the mysterious return of the necklace. I spill the whole story and he looks at me in mouth-open surprised.

"I guess it was more than a math problem, huh?" He punches my arm in a friendly way. "Good going," he says, then puts his earplugs back in.

Mrs. Bliss and I go out to the Medici bakery to celebrate and share an apple croissant. Before we even get there, our mouths are watering from the cinnamon butter smell that swirls down the street. I'm opening the door when Shane comes out carrying a bag.

"Hey, Blue," he says with a friendly nod. I give him a "hey" back, and then he says something else.

"You think maybe we could go to the upper grade social together?"

Of course, I say "yes."

"Good," he says as he smiles and nods. Yvonne is just going to die when she hears.

Mrs. Mansard calls when I get home. She sounds a little frantic. It turns out the student who was living with them and did most of their babysitting had some family emergency and moved out suddenly. Not only do they need a babysitter that night, but are going to need someone on a regular basis from now on.

I tell her I'm her girl right away.

Mr. Mansard picks me up because his wife is still getting ready. When I get to their house, Mrs. Mansard and Boo come down the stairs to the living room. Mrs. Mansard is holding the trick box.

"I was looking for something different to wear and I thought there might be something in here. But I can't remember how to open it." She hands it to her husband. He plays around with it and figures out that one side is a sliding panel. When he opens the panel, the top springs loose. I can't wait to see what's really inside.

Mrs. Mansard takes out some pearl earrings and a locket. Then she lifts out a black and blue beaded necklace with little gray metal things hanging off of it.

"I forgot all about this," she says. "It's not right for me, but Blue, it might be perfect for you."

She says she got it at the Suq and that it was made by the archaeology students. She says the little metal things are an Egyptian version of hearts. When I try it on, it fits perfectly. She says to consider it mine.

When the Mansards leave, I make a Blizzard for Boo. We make hers with frozen strawberries instead of blueberries and call it a Boo Blizzard.

I can tell babysitting for them is going to be great.

Whew. Things are definitely getting better. Nefertiti's necklace is back where it belongs and I'm out of trouble. My economic future is looking up, too. Now, all I have left between me and happiness is the stupid soybean report.

Monday morning rolls around too quickly. My report is as ready as it's ever going to be. Miss Hooper gives me a funny look when I come in to class dragging a box on a luggage carrier I borrowed from Mrs. Bliss.

I got this idea while watching Chef Randy's weekend round up Saturday night. Mrs. Bliss lent me a bunch of stuff, and I raided my money jar to buy the rest of the supplies.

"Well, Blue," Miss Hooper says. "Why don't we just get your report out of the way first thing."

I notice a man and woman in suits sitting in the back of the room. I figure they must be somebody's parents still here from a conference.

I wheel the cart to the front and start unloading. Miss Hooper is watching with her arms folded.

I begin by talking about how soybeans grow and I can see the whole class get a bored look.

"You can hear lots of stuff about soy products like they're the Cinderella of foods, but until you try them..."

I open the box on the luggage cart and set up the blender. I put on the white apron I made out of some dish towels Mrs. Bliss gave me. I take out a bag of frozen blueberries and a bunch of bananas and a brown bottle of vanilla. Finally, I take out the carton of soy milk. I hear a few "yucks" coming from the class when they see what it is.

"Blue, what are you doing?" Miss Hooper says as I pour some soy milk in the blender. "This isn't what your report was supposed to be." She goes on talking about charts and graphs, information, and illustrations. "If you notice, I didn't mention demonstrations," she says in a mean tone.

I freeze. As usual, just when I thought I'd come up with a great idea, it turns out I'm wrong. I guess even if you lose a grade you can't get any lower than an F.

"Excuse me," a woman's voice says from the back of the room. It's the woman in the dark suit. She comes up and talks to Miss Hooper. I can only hear part of it. Something about letting me finish and not crushing creativity.

Miss Hooper's eyes aren't friendly when she turns to me and tells me I can continue.

I measure in the blueberries, cut in the bananas and use a spoon for the vanilla. I turn on the blender and tell them I call this drink a Bean Blizzard. While I let it blend, I explain how some people think soybeans are like a vegetable dairy. I tell them how besides soy milk, there is soy cheese, and even soy ice cream. When it's ready, I pour it into tiny cups so there is enough for everyone. Yvonne offers to help pass them out, and Miss Hooper doesn't give her a problem.

But then everybody turns them down. Yvonne stops and shakes her head. She takes one of the cups and drinks it. Everybody's watching her.

"Wow, Blue it's great," she says wiping away a tiny purple moustache. You can tell by the way she says it, she really means it. Suddenly everybody wants to try it. Even the man and woman in the back. Even Miss Hooper.

I wish I could say I ended up with an A and lived happily ever after. But things never turn out like that for me. The man and woman are from the school board. And even though they like my report and think it's original. Miss Hooper reminds them it's late. She waits until they leave, then tells me I got a C.

But everyone in the class, including Samantha Parker, thinks it was great. Even Denzel stops calling me Bean Fart Blue and changes it to Blue the Bean Queen.

And there's always next time. Miss Hooper announces our next report is supposed to be on an animal.

I think I'll do aardvarks.

BLUE'S RECIPES

Since I'm always talking about cooking, I thought I would include some of my favorite recipes. I have been cooking for a while, so I can do it myself. But if you're new to cooking, it's a good idea to get help from someone older. Also, I always start by washing my hands.

—Blue

BLUE'S OATMEAL COOKIES
FOR PEOPLE WHO DON'T LIKE RAISINS

It is important that you follow the steps of this recipe. If you put all the ingredients in the bowl at the same time, you're going to end up with sludge instead of cookie dough.

1 cup of butter—that means two sticks of REAL butter. I like to take this out of the refrigerator before I start baking so it can get soft. It's much easier to mix then.

¾ cup of white sugar—use a MEASURING cup, not the kind you drink cocoa from.

¾ cup of brown sugar—you have to keep pushing it down as you put it in the measuring cup so it kind of looks like a solid piece.

2 eggs—break these into a little bowl in case some of the shell falls in, then you can pick it out before you add them to the cookie dough.

1 teaspoon of baking soda—be sure to use a MEASURING teaspoon, not the kind you eat with.

½ **teaspoon salt**—same kind of teaspoon as above.

2 teaspoons REAL vanilla extract—by now you know which kind of teaspoon to use.

2 cups of flour

2 cups of oatmeal—don't use the instant kind. It has to be either the old-fashioned or quick kind.

1 cup of sweetened dried cranberries

1 cup of chopped walnuts

What cooking tools you'll need—a big bowl, two smaller bowls, an electric mixer, a scraper, a measuring cup, a set of measuring spoons, a spatula (it's the thing you use to turn pancakes or flip fried eggs) to take the finished cookies off the cookie sheet, and of course, a cookie sheet.

What to do:

1. Set the oven to 350 degrees so it can be heating up while you mix the cookie dough. (If you're not used to using the oven, it's a good idea to get some help from your parents.) Take out your cookie sheet. It's nice if you have two. Take a little slice of butter on a paper towel and rub it over the cookie sheet. This is called greasing it.

2. You can use a round ended knife to cut the sticks of butter into smaller pieces in the mixing bowl. (They don't have to be real tiny pieces. This is just to make it easier to mix them.) Next pour in the white sugar and the brown sugar. Now turn on the mixer and move it around to blend the butter and sugar together. It's mixed enough when it

looks all creamy. Stop the mixer and scrape down the sides of the bowl with the scraper, then mix the stuff from the sides in and turn off the mixer again.

3. Crack the eggs into a small bowl and check for any pieces of shell. If there are any, get rid of them, then pour the eggs into the butter-sugar mixture. Add the vanilla and then turn on the mixer again. It will look kind of oozy at first, but when the eggs get mixed in, it will look a little fluffy. Turn off the mixer.

4. Now mix the flour, oatmeal, baking soda and salt in a different bowl. Then add it by the cupful to the butter-sugar-egg mixture and use the electric mixer after each cupful to blend it all together. You can scrape the bowl whenever it looks like too much stuff is sticking to the sides. When all the dry stuff has been added, turn off the mixer. Add the dried cranberries and walnuts all at once, then use the scraper or a big spoon to mix them in. Even though the cookie dough looks really good, don't taste any because the raw eggs in it could make you sick. Of course, once the cookies are baked, they're fine.

5. I like to use a melon-baller Mrs. Bliss found in her kitchen to put the cookie dough on the cookie sheet, but you can use a teaspoon (the kind you eat with). You take a rounded spoonful of dough and put it on the sheet. But be sure and leave some space between because the cookies spread out when they bake.

6. When you have one sheet full or if you have two, both full, they go in the oven. You bake them from 10–12 minutes.

7. Check them after 10 minutes. They're done when the bottoms are golden. It's a good idea to have some help with this oven part. Always make sure to use a hot pad or something to protect your hand when you take the cookie sheet out of the oven. When they're done you use the spatula to take them off the cookie sheet and put them on a plate. Let them cool a little before eating, if you can stand to wait.

This recipe makes about six dozen cookies.

BLUE'S BLUE BLIZZARD

1 cup milk—use the measuring kind of cup.

1 cup frozen blueberries

1 ripe banana—ripe ones are yellow with a little brown, the more brown spots the sweeter the banana.

1 teaspoon REAL vanilla—use the measuring kind of spoon.

What cooking tools you'll need—an electric blender and a glass.

What to do:

Pour the milk into the blender. Add the blueberries. Break up the banana in pieces and add it to the blender. Pour in the vanilla last. Put the lid on. Turn on the blender. Sometimes the blueberries get stuck on the blender blades and nothing seems to be getting mixed. If that happens, turn off the blender, and take the top off. Stir everything around with a spoon. Take the spoon out, replace the top of the blender and turn it back on. The drink is done when all the bumps of blueberries disappear.

Makes a drink for one.

BLUE'S BEAN BLIZZARD

1 cup vanilla soy milk—the measuring kind of cup.

1 cup of frozen blueberries or frozen strawberries

1 ripe banana—see above for how to tell if it's ripe.

1 teaspoon REAL vanilla—by now I think you know what kind of spoon to use.

You'll need the same electric blender and glass you need for the Blue Blizzard.

What to do.

Pour the soy milk into the blender. Then add the frozen blueberries or strawberries. Break the banana in pieces (of course, peel it first) and add to everything. Now blend. See above for what to do if it looks like nothing is getting mixed.

Personally, I like the Bean Blizzard better than the one made with regular milk. It is so cool to get milk from a bean.

Makes a drink for one. When I made it for my class, I doubled the recipe and just gave them little tastes.

NUTTY POPCORN BALLS

12 cups of popped popcorn—I hope you know the right kind of cup to use by now.

½ cup of sugar (If you measure the sugar first, you won't have to wash out the measuring cup before you measure the molasses.)

1 cup of mild-flavored molasses (After you pour the molasses, be sure to wipe off the rim of the bottle with a damp paper towel. Otherwise, the top will stick, and you'll have a VERY hard time getting it off again.)

4 tablespoons of REAL butter—a tablespoon equals three measuring teaspoons.

1 teaspoon REAL vanilla—remember it's the measuring kind of spoon.

1 cup Spanish peanuts—they're the little round ones with the brown skin.

What cooking tools you'll need—a saucepan, a candy thermometer (I got mine at a rummage sale) or a cup of really cold water, a wooden spoon, a big bowl to put the popcorn in. And if you want to wrap your popcorn balls, you'll need waxed paper or plastic wrap.

What to do:

1. First, measure the popped popcorn into the big bowl and set aside. Put the sugar and molasses and butter into the sauce pan. Stir it all together. The sugar and molasses will mix; the butter will melt when you cook it. Clip the candy thermometer on the inside of the pan so it doesn't touch the bottom. Turn on the stove burner to medium. Cook the mixture until the candy thermometer says 270 degrees.* It is a good idea to stir it every now and then. Don't worry if it looks like something a witch might be cooking, it really tastes good.

   *If you don't have a candy thermometer, there's another way to get the molasses mixture to the right temperature. After you stir the pan, let most of the syrup on the spoon drip back, but also drip a little into the cup of cold water. When the molasses reaches 270, the drop in the water will form a ball that keeps its shape when you take it out of the water. It will feel a little bit like a firm marshmallow. If the drop doesn't keep its shape, cook the mixture a little longer and try again.

2. As soon as the mixture reaches 270 degrees, take the pan off the stove. Add the vanilla and nuts to the molasses mixture and stir it around. Then pour it all over the popcorn. Since it's very sticky, you might need to use a scraper to get it all out. Use the wooden spoon to stir the popcorn so it all gets coated.

3. Now, let it cool. When it is just warm, wet your hands
   (that's so the coated corn won't stick to them) and make
   the balls. I like to do the wrapping when they're all done.

These are so good even my brother-the-brain likes them.

It's hard to say how many balls you'll get because it all
depends on how big you make them. If you make balls about the
size of a tennis ball, you'll get around 32. If you want to, you can
just leave it in the bowl and it turns into one giant popcorn ball
that you can break pieces off of.

FRENCH TOAST AND FRIED BANANAS
FOR YOU AND A FRIEND

3 slices of any kind of bread

2 eggs

1 tablespoon milk—I hate to keep repeating myself, but remember to use a measuring spoon.

1 teaspoon REAL vanilla

2 bananas—the more brown marks on the skin, the riper it is and the sweeter.

3 slices of REAL butter

What cooking tools you'll need—a frying pan. I like to use the non stick kind. A flat bowl to mix the eggs. A spatula to flip the French toast and turn the banana slices.

What to do:

1. Break the eggs into the flat bowl. It's a good idea to check to see if you dropped any pieces of egg shell in with them. If you did, pick them out with a spoon. Take a fork and mix the eggs together until they turn a nice yellow. Add the milk and vanilla and mix some more.

2. Take a slice of bread with a fork and dip it in the egg mixture and turn it so you get both sides. Set it on a plate. Do the same with the other two pieces.

3. Take one of the slices of butter and put it in the frying pan. Turn on the burner and let the butter melt and get kind of brown and bubbly. Put two of the pieces of bread in whole and slice the other one in half so it will fit in the pan. As soon as the bread gets brown squiggly marks on the side facing down, turn the pieces over and add the second slice of butter. When the side facing down gets the brown marks, it's done. Turn off the burner and put the pieces of French toast on two plates.

4. Take the last slice of butter and put it in the pan. Turn the burner back on. As the butter is melting, slice the bananas into the pan. Keep turning over the little banana slices until they get some little brown marks and kind of glisten. Turn off the burner and put some of the banana slices on each of the plates.

I like my French toast plain. But some people like to put syrup on it.

Betty Hechtman grew up in Chicago and babysat her way through school. Along with cooking for the kids she was babysitting, she made up stories for them, too. She still spends a lot of time in Chicago, but her permanent home is in California. The family cat is named Einstein, and the terrier mix is named Goldy Lox. Betty loves kick boxing, indoor cycling, aerobics and yoga, and she recently started crocheting and knitting. She also loves hiking in the nearby mountains. And of course, reading and baking.

If you'd like to write to her, her email address is bettyjhmystery@aol.com.

Home to the Sea

by
Chester Aaron

HOME TO THE SEA
Chester Aaron

Sunday. Midnight.

Marian stirred beneath her thin blanket and sat up.

Quick sharp stabs of cold air brought a flush to her face. Why was she so alert?

Something or someone had wakened her, had been calling to her to get out of bed.

Beyond where Mrs. Kearns' cot would have been, Marian saw the sliding glass door and the darkness beyond.

There! The call came again.

Marian slipped free of her blanket.

The usually noisy floorboards were silent as Marian crossed the room and silently opened the sliding door. Outside, the howling wind that had been rattling the windows a moment before was now an ally, grown suddenly quiet as she left the oceanfront house.

Marian picked her way through beds of dried grass, avoiding the rocks that could bruise a toe or turn an ankle.

There!

From the dark space below the call came again.

She hurried toward the sound, descending through the terraced beds of shrubs and weeds toward the path cut long ago into the side of the cliff.

The next call, hurled forward by the wind, was louder than the sound of the surf pounding the beach below. Marian moved toward that sound as if it was pulling her out from the land.

With the agility of a cat, Marian was up and over the fence and then running, sliding down the path.

Standing finally on a flat shelf of rock above the sand, she looked down at the tide rolling toward her and the surf foaming in the light of the moon and stars. She breathed in the scent of the ocean. Had the ocean ever smelled or tasted so sweet, so delicious, so nourishing?

She stepped down from the rock shelf to the sand. The receding tide caught and pulled her feet from under her. She sat and slid on the thick mud-slush to firm foam-washed sand where she could stand up. She walked toward the breaking surf, pulling off her nightgown and tossing it back over her head. Naked, she ran across the sand until the incoming tide reached her ankles and then her knees. She arched her body and entered the advancing waves headfirst, arms at her sides. Her laughter, like a sang, greeted the ocean as if it were a more familiar force in her life than land had ever been.

There!

The calls were closer now and clearer, variations of pitch and tone that rose, more distinct, above the sounds of surf and wind to form an almost solid tapestry of nonhuman voices that floated across the waves.

HOME TO THE SEA

·································

*"…this myth-novel will pull readers along with its
entrancing story…"* —KIRKUS DISCOVERIES

*"This unusual tale would be a good choice for swim
fans or anyone interested in the legends of mermaids…"*
—SCHOOL LIBRARY JOURNAL

*"Aaron skillfully weaves an uncanny tale of suspense,
family secrets, relationships and love. By adding an
enchanting mixture of fantasy and comedy, he comes
up with a novel that keeps the reader on tenterhooks…
A novel that one would love to return to again and
again…"* —BOOKWIRE REVIEW

HOME TO THE SEA   soft cover $8.95
ISBN: 0974648124, 9780974648125
Available from your bookseller or from the publisher.
Brown Barn Books   *www.brownbarnbooks.com*

THE SECRET SHELTER
Sandi LeFaucheur

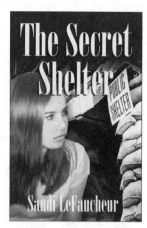

...I pushed the door. No good. Wouldn't budge. With a strength born of fear and fury, I heaved my skinny shoulder against it, once, twice, until on the third try, it burst open. Below me, Marina and Quigs let out a cheer.

The bright sunlight dazzled me after the dusty gloom of the shelter. I closed my eyes briefly and reopened them, grabbing the doorpost for support as the world churned around me. Everything was the same—and yet, different. There was our school, just as before—but different. The window frames were painted brown, not white. Brown tape crisscrossed each pane of glass. High walls of sandbags guarded the entrance to the shelter. In the distance, a line of silvery blimps floated in the sky, bouncing on their tethers. Barrage balloons?

"Sophie?" Marina called from below. "Sophie, are you okay?"

My voice came out as a thin croak from my dry throat. "I'm okay, Marina. But...the world isn't. I...I...something's happened. I don't know what, but something's happened. I stepped outside as Marina and Quigs ran up the stairs.

"It's a joke. Someone's playing a prank. It's a good one, too." Quigs laughed.

Marina scowled at him. "Don't be silly. Who could do this? Who'd paint the school, just as a joke? Pile those sandbags there? Change everything?" Her voice faltered. My hand found hers and we clung to each other. "What's going on, Sophie?"

Praise for THE SECRET SHELTER

Sophie Pinkerton, a high school student growing up in present-day London, shares both a curiosity and history assignment with her friends about what their neighborhood would have been like during World War II.

"Leave the past alone," warns old Mr. Martin, who seems to have a special knowledge of what may await them. However, Sophie, Marina, Quigs, and their teacher, Mr. Schmidt, insist on exploring the old air-raid shelter buried on the school grounds, and find themselves transported back to 1940, , where they meet Quigs's ancestors. The danger is great from both the cruelties of war and the possible discovery of their true identities, especially for German-bom Mr. Schmidt.

LeFaucheur has written a real page-turner, somewhat akin to Jane Yolen's The Devil's Arithmetic (Viking, 1988), and the resolution of the story contains some imaginative twists. Even minor characters are. well developed and interesting, and the historical facts are woven seamlessly into the story. Excellent for "what if" discussions. —SCHOOL LIBRARY JOURNAL

THE SECRET SHELTER   soft cover $8.95
ISBN: 0974648140, 9780974648149
Available from your bookseller or from the publisher.
Brown Barn Books   *www.brownbarnbooks.com*